Silhouettes, Shadows, and Sunsets

Nina and Manny
Summer Lake Silver Book Five

By SJ McCoy

A Sweet n Steamy Romance

Published by Xenion, Inc

Copyright © 2020 SJ McCoy

Published by Xenion, Inc.
First paperback edition 2020
www.sjmccoy.com

This book is a work of fiction. Names, characters, places, and events are figments of the author's imagination, fictitious, or are used fictitiously. Any resemblance to actual events, locales or persons living or dead is coincidental.

Cover Design by Dana Lamothe of Designs by Dana

Editor: Mitzi Pummer Carroll
Proofreaders: Aileen Blomberg, Traci Atkinson, Marisa Nichols

ISBN: 978-1-946220-75-2

Dedication

For Sam. Sometimes, life really is too short. Few oxo

Chapter One

"Hey, Nina. See that guy looking through the window? Is that Brian?"

Nina's heart sank. She knew before she spotted him. An icy finger of dread slid down her back when she saw him, and his gaze locked with hers. She turned away quickly. "Yep."

Janet shuddered. "I am so sorry that I ever set you up with him."

"It's hardly your fault, is it?"

"It's all my fault. You told me you didn't want to go. And I thought I knew better. Thought it'd do you good. Instead of brightening your days with some fun, I landed you with your very own stalker."

Nina glanced at the storefront again, but if Brian was still out there, she could no longer see him. "He's hardly a stalker." She didn't like to think of it that way; that sounded far too sinister. He was just a guy she'd gone on a couple of dates with who was still hoping for another—even though she'd told him no.

Janet blew out a sigh. "Well, next time I see him I'm going to tell him that I don't want him hanging around the store. And I'll remind him that you don't want to see him."

"Thanks. Hopefully, he'll get the message soon and give up."

"I hope so, but if he keeps it up, I'm going to make a complaint about him, report him."

"Who would you even report him to?"

"The police, of course! We need to have it on record in case …"

Nina's heart pounded in her chest. "In case what? In case I turn up as a corpse in the woods?"

Janet laughed. "No! That's not what I meant."

"Good." Nina let out a shaky laugh. "It just sounded like … I don't know. Let's forget about him, can we? He's gone."

"Let's hope that's the last we'll see of him."

Nina nodded. "We can hope. Anyway, what are you doing after we close up?"

"I don't have any plans. Do you want to get dinner at the café?"

"Sure. They'll only be doing the Christmas menu for another week; we might as well get it while we can."

They didn't close up until a quarter after six. It amazed Nina that the Christmas in July sale brought so many people into town. The store had been crazy busy all month. Even though it had died down a little over the last few days, Janet said it had been the best month of the year already.

They managed to get a table outside at the café; it had cooled down enough that the evening air was pleasant.

"How's Abbie doing?" asked Janet after they'd ordered.

"She's doing great. She's loving her job at the medical center, and Ivan's the best thing that ever happened to her. I'm grateful every day that he came into her life."

Janet smiled. "He sounds wonderful. I can't wait to meet him."

"Well, if we could ever take a day off together, you could come back to the lake with me."

"I know, but you've made yourself indispensable in the store. Whenever I take a day off, I like to have you in there."

Nina smiled. She'd only worked at the store since just before Christmas last year, but she felt at home there. She knew she did a good job and was proud that Janet considered her to be her second-in-command.

"Are you going back there at the weekend?"

"Yes. I want to surprise Abbie. I need to make one more check to be sure that the house is ready. I want to get a few more things out, too. From what Austin said, the guy wants to rent it for the month of August for sure, but then he wants to play it by ear after that. If he decides he wants to stay on another month, I won't be able to go back in for more of my things. So, I need to get everything I want out now."

Janet made a face. "If I were renting my house out, I wouldn't leave any of my belongings there."

"I'm not thrilled about it. But I've brought all my personal stuff up here with me, and everything I wouldn't want a renter using is locked in the big hall closet. It beats having to pay for a storage unit. And with this first renter, in particular, I'm not worried."

"Why's that?"

"He's some old man who's retiring from the FBI."

"Aww. I wonder what he's doing spending a month at the lake by himself?"

"It sounds like he has friends in town. But whatever his reasons, he sounds like the perfect tenant to me."

"Yeah, he's hardly likely to make a nuisance of himself, is he? Are you going to leave here after work on Saturday?"

"I'm not sure yet. I could probably get home before dark if I did, but I might wait and go early on Sunday morning. Don't worry, though. No matter when I go, I'll be back in time to open up on Tuesday."

"I'm not worried about you being here. I'm more concerned about there being enough business to keep us all busy."

Nina laughed. "You're kidding? We've been rushed off our feet for weeks."

"Yeah, but once July is over, that's it. August is the quietest month of the year."

"Of course." It'd been easy to get caught up in the madness of the sale, but it was hardly realistic to expect brisk business year-round in a Christmas store. Nina met her friend's gaze. "Will there be enough work for all three of us?"

"All we can do is hope so."

She'd been hoping for a more reassuring answer than that. "What happens if not?"

Janet shook her head. "I don't want to think about it."

"Let's hope we don't have to, then."

"I'm glad you've managed to rent your house out. At least you'll have some money coming in from that."

Nina frowned. It was true that the rent would help out a little, but it sounded as though Janet was saying she might not have a wage to depend on. She hadn't been expecting that. "What do you normally do in August?"

"Jess used to take August and September off."

Nina's heart sank. "So, you're not used to having to pay two salaries through the quiet months?"

Janet shook her head. "Don't worry. We'll work something out."

"I don't suppose Kerry needs any time off, does she?"

"No. And you know she's been with me for years."

Nina was starting to feel uncomfortable now. "Are you trying to tell me that you might not need me?"

"I don't want to tell you that. I hope it's not the case."

"But it's possible?"

Janet nodded slowly. "I'm sorry. I should have warned you sooner, shouldn't I? I just kept thinking that it'd all work out okay—and it might."

"Perhaps so, but you know I'm not exactly in a position where I can just not work for a couple of months."

"I know. I'm sorry."

Nina blew out a sigh. "We'll just have to keep our fingers crossed."

As she walked back to the apartment above the store after dinner, Nina had to wonder whether keeping her fingers crossed was going to be enough. She was disappointed and a little angry that Janet hadn't mentioned this to her before. There were only a few days of July left. If she wasn't going to get enough hours working in the store in August, she'd need to find something else. Her best hope of doing that would be back at Summer Lake—it was the height of the tourist season there. She'd no doubt be able to pick up some hours cleaning at the resort, but since she hadn't known she might need to be there, she'd rented her house out for the month. She shook her head as she dug her keys out of her purse.

As soon as she stepped into the alleyway at the side of the store, she could feel the hairs on the back of her neck stand up. There was someone there. She started to back away.

"Nina!" He stepped out of the shadows and caught her wrist. "I've been waiting for you."

"Brian. What are you doing here?" She pulled back, but his grip tightened.

"I told you. I've been waiting for you."

"Why?" She hated that her voice sounded shaky.

"Because I want to see you." He sounded reasonable enough; his smile was friendly, but there was something in his eyes as he let his gaze travel over her that made her stomach churn.

She backed away as far as she could, just a few more steps would take her out of the alley and back into the street where there was at least some hope of someone seeing her and coming to help.

He started to pull her toward him. "Come here."

"Brian, no!"

He turned her and backed her against the wall, pushing her against it so hard that the air rushed out of her lungs.

"But Nina, yes." He looked like a wolf as he smiled down at her.

Her heart was pounding in her chest, and it shuddered to a halt when his hand slid between her legs. What the …? This couldn't be happening! But it was. A surge of adrenaline gave her a strength she didn't know she possessed. She put both hands in the middle of his chest and shoved as hard as she could. Then she sprinted out of the alley and barreled straight into someone walking down the sidewalk.

A strong hand caught her arm, making her finally find her voice and scream as she pulled away.

"Hey, calm down. Are you okay?" The guy let go of her and held both hands up in the air. "I'm not going to hurt you."

"*He* is!" She pointed back at the alleyway. The guy's companion ran to it and then disappeared.

"Are you okay? What happened?"

Her breath was coming in short, sharp gasps now. She was safe. She nodded. "I'm okay. He … He …" She didn't know what to say. She didn't know what to think. What had happened? Brian had pushed her up against the wall; he'd put his hand between her legs … what would have happened if she hadn't managed to get out of there? She shuddered.

The guy was watching her. "Do you need the police?"

She nodded slowly, remembering what Janet had said earlier about needing to make a report, in case … She shivered. She wasn't going to give him the chance to do anything worse than he already had.

Manny let himself into his apartment and threw his keys and wallet down on the counter. He probably didn't need another drink, but he poured himself a whisky anyway and took it out onto the balcony. It'd been a pleasant evening. He'd attended plenty of parties like that over the years—retirement parties. Up until a few months ago, though, he hadn't thought about having one of his own. He didn't feel old enough to retire; he wasn't old enough, not really. He was fifty-seven. Most people didn't think of that as retiring age. But then, most people weren't special agents.

He took a sip of his whisky. He was no longer Special Agent in Charge of the FBI's Sacramento Field Office. He pursed his lips. He hadn't yet figured out how he felt about that. A part of him had been looking forward to this day, looking forward to being his own person—to being just plain Manny Alvarado, or at least to figuring out who Manny Alvarado might be. Another part of him had been dreading this. What was he going to do with himself?

He knew what he was going to do with the first month of his retirement. And when he managed to relax about it, he was looking forward to it. He was going to spend the month at Summer Lake. It was a quiet little town up in the hills. He had some friends up there. He was hoping to make more, hoping that perhaps he'd find that he fit in there and wanted to stay. He blew out a sigh. If not … well, if not, he'd have to reassess and make a new plan.

He pulled his phone out of his pocket when it rang and smiled when he checked the display.

"Diego!"

"Manny! Congratulations!" He laughed. "Is that the right thing to say? Congratulations on your retirement?"

Manny laughed with him. "Thanks. I think. I'm not sure if congratulations or commiserations are in order, but either way, it's done. I'm retired."

"Well, I say congratulations. You should celebrate. What are you doing this weekend?"

"Not much. Tying up some loose ends. Getting ready to come up there."

"Why wait? Why don't you come now? Be here for the weekend, have some fun."

Manny frowned as he thought about it.

"What's the problem?"

"No problem. The only reason I didn't plan to come until Tuesday is because that's the first of the month, and that's when I took the rental."

Diego laughed. "I never thought I'd see the day that you let the calendar dictate what you do. Call Austin. Tell him you want the place a few days earlier. It's only standing empty. Get your ass up here and start having some fun."

Manny smiled. "I think I'll do that."

"You should. Call me back and let me know when you're arriving. You should try to get here Friday afternoon; that way, you can come out with everyone on Friday night."

"I'll see what I can do, see what Austin says."

"Well, let me know. And you might as well get used to the idea that you're going to be living here. Tell Austin that you don't plan to leave when September rolls around."

"I don't know for sure yet."

"You keep saying that, but I'm telling you, once we get you here, we're not going to let you leave—and you won't want to. Life is good at the lake. You'll see."

After they hung up, Manny smiled to himself. Diego was right, of course. There was no reason he should wait. No reason at all, and the more he thought about it, the more he liked the idea of packing what he planned to take with him and hitting the road.

~ ~ ~

"You're staying here tonight," Janet nodded emphatically as she spoke. They were sitting in her living room. The two police officers had left a little while ago after taking Nina's statement.

She didn't argue. She had no desire to go back to the apartment. The only way to get to it was through the alley, and she didn't ever want to set foot in there again.

"Are you sure you're okay?"

"I am. Honestly. I think I might be in shock. I just didn't expect …" She shuddered. "I thought you were being overly dramatic this afternoon when you called him a stalker. I didn't for one moment think that he'd … that he'd … do anything."

"Neither did I. I feel terrible. It's all my fault."

"It isn't. It's his fault. I don't know what he was thinking. Up until tonight I thought he was harmless; albeit a bit creepy. I even felt a little sorry for him. There's no way you could have known."

"I know, but I was the one who insisted that you were ready to start dating. I set you up on that app and encouraged you to go to dinner with him. Even after that first time you weren't sure, and I nagged you into agreeing to a second date."

Nina shrugged. "You couldn't have known."

"But still … I hope the police find him soon."

"So do I. I won't feel safe until they do."

Janet pursed her lips.

"What?"

"Do you want to go home?"

"Yeah. I think I do."

"Then go. Go first thing in the morning. And if you want to stay there, I'll understand."

Nina held her gaze for a moment. She couldn't help wondering if Janet was looking for an easy out.

"Don't look at me like that."

"Sorry, but is this your way of getting rid of me?"

"You have to admit that it might be best all around."

Nina blew out a sigh. "I suppose so."

"It will. If you go home … give it some time, it'll be best for everyone. It'll give the police time to find him and charge him or whatever happens with something like this. If nothing else, it'll give him time to forget about you. You won't have to stay in the apartment, won't have to walk through the alley until, I don't know … October?"

Nina's head snapped up. "Are you saying that you want me to take the next couple of months off?"

Janet nodded. "I think that'd be best. Don't you?"

It made sense, or at least it would if Nina hadn't rented her house out. At least, she had a few days to figure out what to do. She'd go home in the morning. She wanted to be in her own home; once she was there and she felt safe, she'd figure out what to do next.

"Do you want to call Abbie?"

"No!" Nina didn't plan to tell her daughter what had happened tonight—or that she wouldn't have a job for the next couple of months. She'd only worry and want to help. Nina didn't want to be a burden to her. She'd get herself home and figure out what she was going to do before she told Abbie anything.

Chapter Two

"Hi Austin, this is Manny Alvarado."

"Oh, hi Manny. How are you? We're looking forward to seeing you up here. Are you ready for your trip?"

Manny laughed. "I'm more than ready. I'm on the way. You know what Diego's like. He's talked me into coming up early, so that I'm there for the weekend. I know I said I didn't want to start the rental until the first, but is there any chance I could get in there early? It's not a problem if not. I'll find somewhere else, take a room at the resort for the weekend, if necessary."

"I'm sure it'll be fine. The owner hasn't lived there in over six months. She told me it was available any time after the middle of July. I can't see there being a problem with you taking it a few days early. I'll give her a call and get back to you. Are you literally on the road now?"

"I am. Once I decide I'm going to do something, I like to get on with it. I'll be there this afternoon, so let me know. I'd like to take the place straight away, but obviously I'll understand if that's not possible."

"I'm sure it'll be fine," said Austin. "I hope it will be. I don't like your chances of getting a room at the resort. It's the height of the season here."

"Oh, of course." Manny hadn't thought about that. Still, it wouldn't be a problem. He knew he'd be able to stay with Diego or even with Diego's son Zack if it came down to it.

"I'll call her now and get back to you."

"Thanks. And you said the owner is a widow?"

"That's right. Her husband died a couple years ago. And then last Christmas she moved away. The house has stood empty since then. Her daughter's still in town, though. She keeps an eye on the place."

"Okay. Well, let me know what they say."

"Will do. I'll call you back as soon as I get hold of her."

Manny knew that the house wasn't anything grand. He didn't mind that. He didn't need much. He only planned to use the place as a base while he found his feet. As Austin had just reminded him, he was fortunate to find anything for the month of August in a resort town like that.

As he drove on, he wondered about the old lady who owned the place. From the pictures he'd seen of the house, he'd guess that she was something of a character. The décor wasn't what he'd expect of an old lady. He had to wonder if she'd redecorated after her husband died. Austin had told him that she'd moved away and that only added to his impression of her as a feisty old bird. She wasn't some feeble old thing staying safe in her home after her husband died; she'd gone off and made a new start for herself. Good for her. He'd probably never meet her, but he would take good care of her house for her.

~ ~ ~

"Give me a call when you get there, won't you?" asked Janet.

"I will."

"Have you spoken to Abbie yet? Told her that you're coming?"

"No. And do me a favor? If she calls the store, don't you tell her either. I don't want her worrying. I want to get back there and figure something out, so that when I do talk to her, it'll be all sorted."

"Okay. Listen, I'm really sorry, Nina."

They were standing beside Nina's car which was all loaded up. She'd packed everything because after the way this had all worked out, she wasn't sure if she'd be coming back. It seemed Janet had noticed that and understood. "It's okay."

Janet wrapped her in a hug. "Is it really? Will you be back?"

"Honestly, I don't know. What happened with Brian shook me up. I'm not sure I'll ever want to stay in the apartment again. And the apartment goes with the job, doesn't it?"

"Yes, but by the time we're busy again—by October—hopefully, all this will be in the past, behind us, and we can get back to the way things were. We did have a great time last Christmas season, didn't we?"

"We did." Even as Nina agreed, she couldn't help feeling that last Christmas had been the only one she would spend here in Stanton Falls.

As Janet waved her off, the look in her eyes told Nina that she knew it too.

~ ~ ~

Austin frowned and hung up. He hadn't been able to get hold of Nina Parsons. He'd tried several times since he spoke to Manny, but her phone just rang and rang. She didn't pick up and it didn't go to voicemail. He had a feeling that there wouldn't be a problem if he let Manny have the keys early and let him have the place for the weekend. But he didn't operate on feelings. He did everything by the book—at the very minimum. Wherever possible, he liked to go the extra mile to make sure that everyone he dealt with came away happy.

Since he couldn't get hold of Nina, he decided to try her daughter, Abbie. Abbie was the one who'd come to him originally about renting the place out. Even if she couldn't give him a definite yes or no on letting Manny move in early, she might be able to tell him how to get in touch with her mom.

He dialed her number and waited.

"Hey, Austin. How are you doing? Are you guys coming out this weekend?"

"Hi, Abbs. I think so. Amber said she wants to go. Will you and Ivan be out?"

"We will. But wait. You weren't calling me about that, were you? You would have called Ivan."

Austin laughed. "Yeah. I guess I would. It's actually about your mom's place."

"Oh. What about it?"

"Well, Manny's coming to town a couple of days early and wants to know if he can move straight in. Your mom said it was available any time after the middle of July. But I don't want to just assume that that's still the case."

"I'm sure it'll be fine. She said she'd taken what she needed last time she was here, and she's not planning on coming back for a while. Why don't you call her?"

"I've tried, but she's not answering. And there's no option to leave her a message."

"Oh, her phone does that sometimes when she's out of range. It's weird. I'll tell you what, I'll try the store where she works and tell her to give you a call."

"Thanks."

"And you should probably tell Manny that he's fine to move straight in. The worst that could happen is that she might think of something she needs from the house. If she does, I could always call him and arrange to go over and get it. I don't see the point in making him wait—or making her miss out on an extra few days rent. Do you?"

"No. That sounds like a plan to me. But hopefully, I'll be able to get a hold of her before he arrives."

"Yeah. I'll call the store now. You should hear from her soon."

~ ~ ~

It was afternoon by the time Nina made it to Summer Lake. She'd spent most of the drive back reliving what Brian had done in the alleyway last night. She shuddered as she waited at the stoplight. She'd enjoyed her time in Stanton Falls, but it felt as though it was over now. She didn't know what she was going to do back at the lake, but figuring something out here felt a lot less daunting than the thought of returning to Stanton. Between what had happened with Brian and the way Janet had been so eager for her to leave, she wasn't sure she'd ever want to go back.

When she'd moved to Stanton, it'd felt like she was making a fresh start, but as she drove through Summer Lake, she wasn't sure that she wanted a new life somewhere else. She just hadn't known how to make a new life here—a life without Paul in it.

As she thought about Paul, her eyes filled with tears. She sniffed and turned off the road into the parking lot of the grocery store. She needed a minute to pull herself together, and while she was here, she may as well pick up some cleaning supplies. The house had stood empty for a while now. She'd keep herself busy over the weekend and get it sparkling and fresh for the old guy who'd be staying there. He might be retiring, but this would still be a new start of sorts for him. She liked the idea of doing what she could to make it a good one for him, and a clean house was all that she could contribute to that.

She jumped when her phone rang, and she fished it out of her purse. There was a voicemail from Janet.

"Hi, Nina. You might still be on the road, but you were supposed to call me and let me know when you got there safely. Abbie called the store looking for you. She wants you to give her a call. Don't worry, I didn't say anything. But you should call her soon, or she'll worry. And don't forget to call me. Okay. Take care."

Nina ended the call and blew out a sigh. She'd have to call Abbie. It was strange that she'd called the store and not her cell, but sometimes she had no signal on the drive back here. Perhaps that was it. She'd have to call her, but she could probably leave it until tomorrow. She didn't want to ruin her Friday night. And maybe by tomorrow she'd have pulled herself together enough that she'd be able to come up with a convincing story about why she was back here. She hardly wanted to tell Abbie—and especially not Ivan—about Brian.

She got out of the car and made her way into the grocery store. She'd pick up something for dinner and everything that she'd need to spend her weekend in a cleaning frenzy that would hopefully help her work her way out of this funk.

As she was coming out of the store, a big smile spread across her face when she spotted her old friend Teresa coming in.

"Nina! What are you doing here?" Teresa looked at the cart. "You got a cleaning job?"

Nina laughed. "Not quite. I'm going to blitz my place this weekend."

Teresa narrowed her eyes. "What are you hiding?"

"What do you mean?"

"I mean, you've been crying, I can tell. You're here when you're supposed to be at your job in Stanton Falls, and you're a compulsive cleaner when you're upset. So, what's going on?"

Nina's eyes filled with tears again. Teresa was a real friend; she couldn't help but compare her to Janet.

"Oh, sweetheart." Teresa wrapped her in a hug. "Come on. You're coming to my place, and you can tell me all about it."

Nina sniffed. "You're about to go shopping."

"Pft. I have priorities, and right now, you're my number one. Come on, I'll see you at my place in ten minutes."

Nina smiled gratefully. "Call it fifteen? I'll drop all this stuff at the house first."

"Okay, but any more than fifteen minutes, and I'll be coming around to get you."

"I'll be as quick as I can. I promise."

"Okay. I'll open us a bottle of wine."

~ ~ ~

Manny pulled the car over into the pullout by the side of the road and let out a low whistle. He'd fallen in love with Summer Lake when he came up here to help out Diego's son, Zack. It was a beautiful place with the mountains huddling around the lake. He'd never stopped to take in the view from up here, though. It was spectacular.

He got out to stretch his legs and pulled his phone out. He'd hoped to have heard back from Austin before now. It was almost five. He decided to give him a quick call to see if he could catch him while he was still at the office. He knew Austin would answer him at any time, but he didn't want to disturb the guy's weekend if he could help it.

"Hi, Manny." Austin answered. "I'm sorry I haven't gotten back to you yet. I was really hoping to hear from Nina this afternoon."

"It's no problem. I'll call Diego and ask if I can stay with him."

"No. You don't need to do that. I did speak to her daughter and she said it would be fine. I'm just being extra cautious."

Austin chuckled. "That's the way I roll. I wanted confirmation from Nina herself, but there's really no need. Abbie said it would be fine, so it will be fine. What time will you be here?"

"I can be at your office in ten minutes if you want to give me the keys."

Austin laughed. "Okay, great. I'll see you when you get here. I'll take you over there."

"That's okay. It's Friday afternoon. Just give me the keys, and I can take it from there."

When he got to the office, Manny could tell that Austin wasn't comfortable leaving him to find the house and let himself in. He was a good kid.

"You can follow me over. I don't need to hang around for long but …" Austin's phone rang, and Manny smiled.

"Go ahead. Take it."

Austin gave him an apologetic smile. "Hey, Amber. Are you okay? … Oh, okay. No … I'm just …" He glanced at Manny.

Manny smiled. "Just give me the keys. I'm fine. I promise I'll call you if I have any issues. Okay?"

Austin pursed his lips for a moment and then relaxed and smiled. "I'll be home in about twenty minutes, sweetie." He hung up and handed Manny a set of keys. "Here you go. It's not like you need me for anything, is it?"

Manny laughed. "I might be retired now, but I think I can handle going into an empty house alone."

Austin chuckled. "Yeah, I guess you can. Are you going to the Boathouse later?"

"Yep. If I don't get there under my own steam, I think Diego may come and drag me out."

"You might have a point there. He's so excited for you to be here. Zack is, too, and Maria, for that matter. You should probably be prepared for a lot of female interest."

Manny laughed. "Maria's a sweetheart. She makes me laugh, going out of her way to pretend that I'm some kind of … good-looking."

Austin raised an eyebrow. "Pretending? She's not pretending, nor are any of the girls who've seen you around town. You have your very own fan club already."

Manny made a face. "I don't know about that. But it sounds like you have a young lady who's eager for you to get home."

"Yeah. I'd better go. I'll introduce you to her later. I'm not sure you met her when you were up here before."

"Amber, right? I think I saw her around, but you weren't together then."

"No," Austin smiled. "It took me a while to get my act together."

"Well, don't blow it now. Get on home to her. I'll see you later."

Manny smiled when he pulled up in front of the house. It was a quiet street, unassuming. Most of the houses were simple ranchers with the occasional Cape Cod here and there. This one was neat and well kept, white with blue shutters. A neat, little front yard was bisected by a path leading to the front door.

As he looked, he was surprised to see a figure moving in the window. The way the sun sat low in the sky, it shone through the windows and silhouetted a female figure—a very attractive female figure—moving around in the kitchen.

He sat there for a few moments smiling to himself. A woman wasn't on his wish list, but something about that one made him wonder why not. He chuckled and got out of the car. He shouldn't be sitting here ogling the cleaner. He should at least go in and introduce himself so that she didn't call in a stalker sitting outside the house.

He pushed the front door expecting to find it open. But it was locked. He got out the key and called as he let himself in.

"Hello?"

There was only silence. He went into the kitchen and saw a bunch of cleaning supplies sitting on the counter, but no cleaning lady to go with them. He went to the back window and saw a car pulling away. Perhaps she planned to come and clean tomorrow and hadn't yet heard of his early arrival. He smiled. If so, that would mean he'd get to meet her when she came back.

He shook his head. He hadn't thought that a woman was on his wish list, but given his eager reaction to the mere silhouette of an attractive cleaning lady, he might have to take a closer look at that list.

Chapter Three

Nina set down her empty wineglass and gave Teresa a rueful smile. "So, there you have it. I'm back at the lake for the foreseeable future."

Teresa shook her head. "I'm surprised at Janet. I expected she'd take better care of you than that."

"It's hardly her fault. She thought she was taking care of me. Encouraging me to put myself back out there and go on a date with Brian. There's no way she could have known that he'd turn out to be …" She shuddered as she remembered the look in his eyes when he'd pushed her up against the wall in the alley. What would he have done if she hadn't managed to get away from him?

Teresa picked up the bottle. "We may as well finish this off."

Nina checked her watch. It was getting late, but it wasn't as though she had to get up for work in the morning.

Teresa poured the last of the wine into their glasses. "I didn't mean Janet should have taken better care of you with that guy. I'm mad at her, but you're right, she couldn't have known. But, by the sounds of it, she knows that she doesn't have enough work to go around in August and September. She should have told you back in the spring. That way you could have set something up back here. They always need help at the resort over the summer, but you know what Ben's like, he sets up the schedule way in advance."

"I know. I'll go and see him tomorrow, see if he can give me any hours, even if it's only emergency cover. I'll take anything I can get at this point."

"What are you going to do about the house? When's the renter supposed to arrive?"

"Tuesday. He's booked for the whole month of August, and Tuesday's the first, so …"

"I know you don't want to stay with Abbie. And I know my spare room isn't ideal, but you're welcome to it if you want it."

"Thanks, Teresa. You're the best."

"It's what friends do … real friends, at any rate."

Nina had to hide a smile at that. Teresa and Janet had been part of her group of friends ever since high school. While she got along with them both, there'd never been any love lost between them. Teresa had been supportive when she'd gone up to Stanton Falls to work for Janet, but cautious, too.

"I appreciate the offer; you know I do. But I want to see what I can figure out for myself. I was so proud of myself working in the store and living in the apartment. I felt like I'd finally found my feet." Tears welled up in her eyes out of nowhere. "That's the first time I've ever lived by myself, you know."

"I know. I remember that first little apartment you and Paul had right out of high school. We were all so jealous. You two had it figured out right from the beginning."

Nina nodded. She used to think so. She and Paul had started dating in her junior year of high school. Paul had graduated a year before her and taken a job working at the auto repair shop down Route 20. They'd married the year after she graduated, bought the house a few years after that, and then, when she was twenty-four, they'd had Abbie.

Teresa touched her arm. "I'm sorry, honey. How are you doing?"

Nina shrugged. "I don't know. I … like I said. I was proud of myself with the job at the store and living in the apartment. I started to find my feet." She took a sip of her wine. "And there's no reason I shouldn't keep moving forward just because I'm back here, is there?"

"No, but I'd guess it's harder here. Harder being back in your house."

Of course, it would be harder, being back in the house she and Paul had shared for nearly thirty years. She smiled at her friend. "I'll only be there for a couple of days. Then I'll have to find somewhere else for at least a month while it's rented out."

"Yeah. And seriously, you're welcome to stay here."

"Thanks."

"Do you have any plans tomorrow night?"

"Other than going to talk to Ben about picking up some hours at the resort, I don't have any plans at all. Why?"

"Well, I heard that Clay McAdam's going to sing with the band tomorrow night. I wouldn't mind going to see him. If you want to?"

Nina thought about it. "Sure. I'll have to talk to Abbie tomorrow, let her know that I'm here. So, I won't be hiding out like tonight."

Teresa laughed. "This is kind of fun though, holing up here drinking wine on a Friday night and catching up."

"It is," Nina agreed. "This is just what I needed. Thanks, Teresa."

"There's no need to say thank you. It's what friends do."

"Well, friends also take each other out for dinner. And I'm treating you tomorrow. Okay?"

"You don't need to do that."

"I know I don't, but I want to." She smiled. "It's what friends do."

It was almost midnight when Teresa walked her out to her car. "Are you sure you don't want to stay the night?"

"No. Thanks, but I want to get started cleaning early in the morning. Give me a call, though, let me know what time you want to meet up for dinner?"

"Okay." Teresa frowned. "Do you want me to follow you back over to your place? Make sure you get home safe?"

Nina smiled. "I'll be fine. I don't mind telling you I was creeped out up in Stanton, but being back here ..." She shrugged. "It's Summer Lake. Bad things don't happen here."

She drove the short distance back from Teresa's and pulled the car into the space around the back of the house. She hesitated for a moment before she got out. Bad things really didn't happen here. She knew that, but it didn't stop her from hurrying up the path to the back door or locking it quickly behind her once she was inside.

She let out a nervous chuckle as she turned the kitchen light on. She was just giving herself the jitters. Her heart leaped into her mouth when she spotted movement outside the window. It couldn't be? Brian wouldn't have followed her here, would he?

She turned the light off again quickly. She couldn't see out into the dark yard, but if he was out there, she didn't want him to be able to see her either. She peered out into the darkness, but nothing moved. Perhaps it was her own reflection that had caught her eye?

She didn't know, but she didn't want to take any chances. She opened the top drawer in the cabinet next to the fridge. There was a flashlight in there somewhere. She could use that to make her way upstairs, then she'd lock the bedroom door behind her. She was probably being silly, but there was no harm in being cautious. She rummaged around in the drawer, wondering where on earth the flashlight was.

"Stop!" A deep, commanding voice made her jump

Her heart felt like it was exploding in her chest, and she scrabbled in the drawer for anything she could use as a weapon to defend herself. She didn't find anything before a large pair of arms closed around her.

Finally, her brain kicked in and she screamed. "No! Brian, no!"

"Brian?" The arms tightened around her and some part of her brain registered that they were much bigger, more muscular, than Brian's arms.

She closed her eyes and tensed. She might have been able to push Brian away, but the way this guy was holding her, she knew that there'd be no getting away from him.

"What are you doing?"

She opened her eyes slowly, wondering why it mattered.

He gave her a shake. "What are you doing here?" He asked again.

"I … I don't understand."

The man blew out a sigh and loosened his grip on her. He kept hold of one arm as he moved away and … flicked on the light switch.

Nina blinked as her eyes adjusted to the light and to the sight of the man in front of her. He must have scared her out of her wits because all she could think about was how handsome he was! He was tall, maybe six feet. Muscular, olive-skinned with dark hair, liberally sprinkled with gray.

He was glaring at her. "What are you doing here?"

It seemed that the third time of asking was the charm. She finally found her voice and was grateful when it came out sounding much stronger than she felt. "I live here. What are you doing here?"

He let go of her arm and stepped back. "You … live here?"

Nina started to back away from him, seeing her chance to escape.

He looked pale. "I'm so sorry. Are you Abbie?"

Now she was thoroughly confused. "Why? What do you know about Abbie?"

He shook his head as if to clear it. "She's the … you're not …"

"Abbie's my daughter."

"You're Nina Parsons?"

She nodded. "Who the hell are you?"

"I'm so sorry. I'm Manny. Manny Alvarado."

She stared at him for a long moment. "You're the renter?"

He nodded. "I thought you were breaking in."

"I thought you were …" She didn't know how to finish that sentence, so she didn't even try.

Manny's heart rate was slowly returning to normal as he processed what was going on here. He'd had a good night at the Boathouse with Diego and Izzy and their friends. He'd been trying to get to sleep when he'd heard movement downstairs and come to investigate.

He held the woman's gaze. The fact that she was beautiful wasn't what he should be registering right now, but he couldn't seem to move past it. Her dark hair framed her face, her eyes were big and brown … and they were still filled with fear.

He held both hands up in the air. "I'm so sorry." It was bad enough that he'd grabbed her in her own kitchen, but the worst part had been her reaction. She screamed Brian, no! Who the hell was Brian, and what had she thought he was going to do to her?

She gave him a weak smile. "It's okay." Then her smile faded, and she looked suspicious. "What are you doing here again? Why are you visiting?"

Manny was proud of her for checking his story—though of course, he couldn't tell her that. "I just retired, from the FBI." He knew that last detail would work in his favor.

She nodded. "I thought you'd be older—with you retiring."

He risked a smile. "If it's any consolation I feel old, but mandatory retirement age is fifty-seven."

"Wow. That's young."

He nodded. "I thought you'd be older, too."

She frowned, and he realized that he didn't want to explain why; he'd heard she was a widow and immediately imagined her as an old lady. She was only his age—he'd guess maybe a few years younger. Her husband must have died young.

She blew out a shaky breath. "Well, now that you know I'm not a burglar and I know you're not …" She shuddered. "… what I thought you were. Do you want to tell me what you're doing here? You're not supposed to arrive until Tuesday."

"I called Austin, he said it'd be okay to arrive early. He checked with your daughter—she said the same. They did try to get hold of you."

He was surprised to see the hint of a smile on her lips. "I didn't tell anyone I was coming. I wanted to surprise Abbie."

He smiled. "Well, you definitely surprised me."

To his relief, she smiled back at him. "I don't mind telling you that you scared the life out of me."

He couldn't help it. He had to ask. "Who's Brian?"

Her smile disappeared, making him wish he'd kept his mouth shut. But when she looked up at him, he saw fear in her eyes, and there was no way he could let that pass.

"Are you okay?"

She nodded. "Do you want a drink?"

"Sure."

She went to the cabinet and poured two glasses of whisky before pulling up a seat at the counter and gesturing for him to do the same.

"He's the reason I'm back here." She visibly shuddered, making Manny want to put his arm around her.

"A boyfriend?" He had to know.

She shook her head. "A bad date." She let out a little laugh. "Well, two bad dates. I didn't even want to go the second time. I told him there wouldn't be a third, but he didn't agree and started following me around. Then he … he …" She pulled herself together and met his gaze. "He tried to grab me last night in the alleyway outside my apartment. I was lucky. I got away from him, and there were some guys passing by who helped."

Manny's heart was thundering in his chest. He knew it happened. It happened all the time, unfortunately, but to think of her being grabbed like that … to think what might have happened if she hadn't gotten away. He took a slug of his whisky. "Thank God they were there."

She nodded. "Yeah."

They were both quiet for a few moments. Manny's mind was racing. He should be thinking about himself, figuring out what he was going to do—he was going to need to find somewhere else to stay—but all he could think about was the woman sitting beside him.

"There's no chance that he'd follow you here, is there?"

She turned big scared brown eyes on him. "God, I hope not."

"But you thought he had. You thought I was him." Damn, that was stupid of him. He hadn't meant to scare her. He should leave it alone. He drained his glass and gave her a rueful smile. "I'd better get out of your hair."

"What … what do you mean?"

He smiled. "Well, I imagine you're going to be staying here, you're going to need your place back." His smile faded. "You're not going back there, are you?"

When she shook her head, he relaxed his grip on the glass.

"Then you're going to need your house—and I'm going to have to find another."

"No!"

She said it so quickly it surprised him. He raised an eyebrow.

"Sorry. But please don't do that. I … I'll be able to find somewhere to stay. My daughter. My friend I visited this evening. I can stay with one of them."

He gave her what he hoped was a reassuring smile. "I wouldn't ask you to give up your place for me. You should be here—in your home—where you feel safe."

"Thank you. I appreciate that. But … honestly …"

Her cheeks turned pink, and he wondered what she was about to say.

"I'd rather you stayed here ... and pay."

Of course. It hadn't occurred to him, but she must need the money. Damn. He was going to be the bad guy either way then. He'd either have to put her out of her home or not pay her the rent money she'd been expecting. Unless ... no, that was a crazy idea. He smiled. It wasn't crazy. It was adjusting on the fly and making the best of a bad situation—he was well known for excelling at that.

He met her gaze, wondering if she'd like the idea or hate it. Would it help her out or scare her silly? There was only one way to find out.

"So, how about we both stay here? I'm happy to pay the rental fee, but I don't need the entire house to myself. I won't be home much ..." He watched her face as he spoke. She wasn't dead against it, but she wasn't sure. He smiled. "And you know, if this Brian character shows up here, I'm not a bad guy to have around."

She searched his face for a moment, and then she relaxed and nodded. "Okay. Thank you"

He smiled back. "Thank you."

Nina locked the bedroom door behind her and sank down onto the bed—Abbie's bed. Of course, Manny had taken the master bedroom—her bedroom—when he arrived. Why wouldn't he? He'd offered to move out of it, but she'd refused. She'd be perfectly fine here in Abbie's room. She wanted to believe that it was about the money—she was going to have to give him some of it back since he was only renting a room now rather than the whole house. But as she climbed into her daughter's bed, she had to admit that wasn't the reason. Manny had just gotten out of her bed and the thought of getting in there where he'd just been … She bit down on her bottom lip. She shouldn't even be thinking like that! Shouldn't be thinking about Manny in her bed … in any sense.

She turned off the light on the nightstand and lay there staring up into the darkness. It'd been two years since Paul died. She hadn't given any thought to being with another man for most of that time. Then in the last few weeks, she'd gone out with Brian—and discovered the worst side of dating—and now she'd met Manny and couldn't stop herself from wondering what it might be like to go on a date with him.

She blew out a sigh. That was crazy. The stress of the last few days must be getting to her. Perhaps she was crazy to even be here? Should she have gone back to Teresa's, or even to Abbie's? How could she feel safe lying here with a strange man staying in her room just down the hall? Especially after Brian?

She blew out another sigh. Crazy or not she knew, just knew in her gut, that she had nothing to worry about with Manny. He made her feel safe. Maybe it was because he was an FBI agent, or maybe it had more to do with his big strong arms and his kind eyes.

She turned on her side and pulled the covers up over her shoulder. She didn't need to be thinking about his eyes. She needed to get some sleep. In the morning, she'd figure out whether or not she was crazy—and when she saw Abbie, she'd no doubt hear her daughter's thoughts on that subject, too.

Chapter Four

Manny opened the bedroom door cautiously. He hadn't heard Nina get up, and he didn't want to disturb her if she was still sleeping. Her door was closed, and he tiptoed past it and headed downstairs.

He stopped when he reached the kitchen. She was already in there. She had her back to him, making coffee. He couldn't help but look her over. She was wearing faded blue jeans and a white shirt with big daisy flowers on it that, for some reason, made him smile.

He cleared his throat wanting to let her know that he was there, but not wanting to startle her. To his dismay, she let out a little yelp and dropped the carafe of water as she spun around.

He held both hands up as he hurried toward her. "I'm sorry. I didn't mean to scare you." He grabbed the roll of paper towels from the counter and started to mop up the mess.

She squatted down at the same time as he did. Her hand brushed his as she used a towel to soak up the water. It was only the slightest touch, but it sent an electric current racing up his arm. His head snapped up, and he sought her gaze, wondering if she'd felt it, too.

Her big brown eyes were wide. Last night he'd seen them filled with fear. Now, though, that wasn't fear in them ... shock, perhaps? He didn't know. Her cheeks flushed, and she looked away before he could figure it out.

"I'm sorry. I'm so clumsy." She picked up the carafe. "At least I didn't break it."

"Please, don't apologize. It was my fault. I startled you."

She shook her head. "That's not your fault. I'm just a bit jumpy."

"And that's understandable."

She nodded. "I know coffee's supposed to make you jittery, but I need the first cup to settle me down."

Manny smiled. "Why don't you make it. Let me clean this up." He reached to take the towel from her hand, and there it went again—the briefest of touches, the overwhelming reaction.

She relinquished the towel and got to her feet without meeting his gaze. "I hope you like it strong?"

He stared at her for a moment, not understanding what she meant. He was liking his strong reaction to her, but he wasn't sure that it was appropriate.

She rinsed the carafe and filled the coffee pot. "I need my coffee strong. We can always add some water to yours if it's too much."

Ah. Of course. The coffee. "I'm sure it'll be fine."

When it was ready, he took the mug she poured for him and smiled. "Thanks."

She nodded. "You're welcome. Can I get you anything else?"

"No. I'm fine, thanks. And I don't want you to feel that you have to take care of me—do anything for me."

She shrugged. "I don't know what to think right now, to be honest. I suppose, if anything, I'm thinking I should probably find somewhere else to stay. Let you have the house, like you expected."

Manny's heart sank. It made sense. His suggestion last night that they should both stay here was hardly conventional. But he liked the idea of it. He didn't want her to leave on his behalf. "I hope you don't."

Her eyes darted toward his, and when they met, he felt like she understood what he meant—even though he wasn't sure that he fully understood it himself.

He shrugged. "I told you I don't need the whole house. I'll do my best not to get in your way."

She smiled, and it encouraged him.

"I only know a couple of people in town. It'd be nice to make another friend."

She met his gaze for a moment before looking away. The way she kept doing that made him wonder if she wasn't feeling the same kind of attraction that he was.

She sipped her coffee and stared out of the window for a few moments.

Manny realized that he was holding his breath while he waited for her to speak. He exhaled when she did.

"Well, if you're sure you don't mind …"

He shook his head. "Really. I don't."

She nodded. "We'll have to work something out. I can't charge you rent when technically, you'd only be a lodger."

He smiled at the term. "The rent was very reasonable—especially for the height of the season. I'm sure you could have asked a lot more and got it."

"We don't have to argue about it right now, but I'm not going to take advantage of you."

Manny had to bite down on his bottom lip to keep in a smile. He wouldn't mind—in fact, he liked the idea of her trying to take advantage of him—though not financially.

She surprised him when she let out a little laugh and her cheeks turned pink again. "Sorry. That sounded wrong. You know what I mean."

He chuckled. "I do." He wanted to say more, let her know what he'd been thinking, but decided against it. It sounded as though she'd been through something of an ordeal with the last guy she'd dated. The last thing he wanted was for her to start seeing him as another creep.

She slid down from her seat. "I know you don't need me to do for you, but I'm going to make myself an omelet. Would you like one?"

"Yes, please." It felt awkward but turning down the offer would feel more so. He pursed his lips. He wanted to suggest that if she was taking care of breakfast, perhaps she'd let him take her to dinner. But that wouldn't be right. He should rein it in. If he was going to be her house-guest or tenant or lodger or whatever the right word was for the whole month, then there'd be plenty of time to figure out how things would work between them.

"What are your plans for the day?" she asked as she pulled a pan from the cabinet.

"I'm going over to see Diego's place later. Do you know him? He and Izzy moved here recently."

"No. I know his son, Zack and his fiancée, Maria. They're friends of Abbie's."

"That's right. Diego's not been here long, and Austin said you've been gone since late last year."

"Yeah. I moved up to Stanton just before Christmas last year."

"What made you move?"

"My friend Janet offered me a job. Stanton Falls is like Christmas town. They go overboard for the holiday season and she needed extra help. Then her oldest employee announced that she was going to retire, so Janet asked me to stay on."

"But now you're done?" He didn't like the idea of her going back there. Not with this Brian character on the loose. He'd have to check in with the sheriff, see what he could find out.

She shrugged as she whisked the eggs. "Yeah. Even without what happened the other night. It turns out that Janet doesn't have enough work to keep me on for the next few months. She won't need me again until October."

"Will you go back then?"

"I don't think I want to."

"But you might?"

"I might need to. I'll have to take whatever work I can find here—I'll probably get some hours at the resort during the season, but there won't be anything in the winter. Janet might be my only option. I don't want to go back there, though."

Manny nodded. It was strange. He didn't know her or know much of anything about her, but he didn't want her to go back there either.

Nina was grateful when Manny left to go and see his friends. It wasn't that she didn't enjoy his company—far from it. The problem was that she was enjoying it a little too much. He was an attractive man—a very attractive man. She blew out a sigh. And that was the last thing she needed to be thinking about. Especially not now, not here—not back in the home that she and Paul had shared for most of her life.

She finished rinsing the dishes and loading them into the dishwasher and then dried her hands. She had things to do today—things to distract her both from the scary guy who'd precipitated her return and the appealing guy she'd found once she got here. Paul's shadow hung over them both. She blinked rapidly, not allowing the tears to come.

She'd have to get hold of Abbie and let her know she was back, even though she wasn't keen to tell her why. She checked the clock on the wall. She'd have time to go over to the resort and see if she could find Ben. If there was any work to be found for her, she knew that Ben would find it.

She picked up her cell phone. She should leave Abbie a message. It was the coward's way out, she knew that, but at least it would give Abbie time to process the fact that she was back here before they talked in person.

To her surprise, it didn't go straight to voicemail.

"Mom?"

"Oh, hi sweetie. I didn't expect you to pick up. I thought you were working."

"I am, but I've been worried about you. Janet sounded shady yesterday, and you didn't call me back. What's going on? I've been worried."

"Everything's okay. There's nothing to worry about. I wanted to surprise you. I'm back. I'm here at the lake."

"Oh! Wow! That's … Wait. When did you get here?"

"Yesterday."

"Where did you stay? That Manny guy's at your house."

"I know." Nina couldn't help smiling to herself. "Everything's okay. Do you want to meet up when you get off work?"

Abbie was quiet for a moment. "What's going on, Mom?"

"Nothing. I just know that you're busy. You're at work. Do you want me to meet you there when you get done?"

"How about you come over to the house? I'll be home just after one."

"Okay, great. I'll see you then. I'll pick us up some lunch if you like?"

"Thanks. That'd be great. I have to go."

"Okay, see you later, love."

"Bye."

Nina ended the call and set the phone back down on the counter. This was ridiculous; she was nervous about what Abbie would say, what she'd think about her letting Manny stay here. She shrugged. She'd understand. She'd have to. As she wiped the counter down, it struck her as odd that she was more concerned what Abbie might think about Manny than what she might think about Brian. She didn't want to examine that too closely. She didn't need to. She needed to get herself ready and get over to the resort, see if she could find Ben.

It was one fifteen by the time she brought the car to a stop in front of the gate at Abbie and Ivan's place. She smiled to herself as she keyed in the code and waited for the gate to roll back. She loved that her daughter lived here; she loved the guy she lived with. Ivan was an absolute sweetheart as far as Nina was concerned. He was perfect for Abbie. And though it had taken them a while to figure that out, they couldn't be happier together since they had. Nina was looking forward to the day they'd get married, and though she didn't dare say as much, she was hoping that the day would come when they'd make her a grandma, too.

Abbie appeared on the steps outside the front door just as Nina brought the car to a stop. She waved when Nina got out and came down to greet her with a hug.

"I missed you, Mom."

"I missed you, too, love. How've you been?"

Her daughter's smile made her heart fill up and overflow. "Great. Everything's wonderful. Ivan, work, this place ..." She turned and looked up at the house. "Life is good, it couldn't be better. I've never been this happy, Mom, I didn't think I ever would be."

Nina pulled her back in for another hug. "I always hoped you would."

"What about you, though?" Abbie stepped back with a frown. "Want to tell me what's going on? Why are you here on the weekend when you should be at work? What's up with Janet? She sounded weird when I talked to her yesterday. And since you avoided the question earlier, where did you stay last night?"

"That's a lot of questions. Aren't you going to invite me in— offer me something to drink?" She reached into the back seat and held up a takeout bag from the resort. "I'll tell you everything you want to know over lunch."

"Okay." Abbie eyed her suspiciously. "But why do I get the impression that there's something going on?"

Nina had to smile. "Probably because you're smart, and there is."

They ate lunch sitting at the table in the nook. The whole house was beautiful, but this was Nina's favorite spot. The windows looked out over the lawns that led down to the lake. She gazed out at the water sparkling in the afternoon sun.

"Come on," said Abbie. "You've put me off for long enough. What's going on?"

Nina blew out a sigh. "I just didn't want to worry you, that's all, love."

"About what?"

"About anything. I'm back because Janet doesn't have enough work for me for the next few months. August and September are the quietest months for her. Kerry's been with her for years, so I was kind of last in, first out."

Abbie frowned. "You never mentioned anything about that before."

"I didn't know about it until the other night."

"Well, she should have let you know sooner than this. Janet's never been my favorite."

Nina had to smile. It was true. Abbie had always been prickly with Janet. Teresa didn't think much of her either. "Well, it seems you're smarter than me. You and Teresa both."

Abbie smiled. "Now, Teresa is my favorite. Did you stay with her last night?"

Nina dropped her gaze.

"No? Mom, I can tell there's something else going on with you. Why don't you just tell me?"

Nina let out a little laugh. "Okay. I will. But don't get mad at me, will you?"

"I can't answer that until I know what I might be mad about—so tell me!"

"Okay. Well, why did you call me yesterday?"

"To tell you about Manny arriving early."

"Yes, but you didn't mention that, did you? You only told Janet that you wanted me to call you. And you didn't mention Manny in the voicemail you left me either."

"No. So…?"

"So, I didn't know that he was coming early."

Abbie frowned.

"So, I stayed at the house last night."

Abbie's eyebrows shot up. "What about Manny?"

"He stayed there too."

"Err … tell me more?"

Nina shrugged. "I had dinner with Teresa. It was after midnight when I got home. I … I thought I saw someone moving around in the yard, so I turned the kitchen light off so that they wouldn't see me. Then I started going through the drawers looking for a flashlight, and Manny—who was already there and had gone to bed—came down and thought I was a burglar."

"What did he do?" Abbie's eyes were wide.

Nina felt her cheeks flush. "He grabbed me and demanded to know what I was doing."

"Oh my God! Mom!"

Nina couldn't help but chuckle. "He scared the life out of me."

"I'll bet." Abbie shot her a look she didn't understand. "What happened then?"

"We figured out what was going on—that I wasn't a burglar, and neither was he …"

"And you went to bed?"

Nina's heart started to race, and she felt her cheeks flush again. "Abbie! No! We … I … He was already set up in my room, and I took yours."

Abbie's eyes narrowed as she held her gaze. "Yeah. That's what I meant … you went to bed."

Nina's heart was still racing. Of course, that was what she'd meant—that they'd each gone to their respective bedrooms and gotten into bed. Not that they'd *gone to bed* with each other. She looked away, pretending to be absorbed in the view of the lake.

"So, what happens now?"

She looked back at her daughter, not wanting to answer until she was sure what the question was this time.

"Where's he going to stay now that you're back? Or where are you going to stay?"

Nina had to swallow before she spoke. There was no reason Abbie should have a problem with it—was there? She was about to find out. "Well, he offered to find somewhere else, to let me have the place back. And I told him that I'd rather he stayed. I'm counting on that rent, Abbs. Especially now I'm not working for Janet."

"You can stay here. You know that."

"There's no need."

Abbie raised an eyebrow and waited. It seemed that she already knew what Nina was about to say.

"I'm staying at the house. He said he doesn't need the whole place, and I don't either."

To her surprise. Abbie smiled. "It makes sense."

"You don't mind?"

"Why would I mind?"

"I thought you might … I don't know … I …"

Abbie reached across and took hold of her hand. "From what I've seen of Manny, he's a great guy. Zack and Maria love him to pieces, and come on, Mom, he's a freaking FBI agent. I like the thought of you having someone like that around." Her lips quirked up into a smile. "And I mean, he's kind of easy on the eyes, too, right?"

Nina tried to hide her smile. "I hadn't noticed."

Abbie laughed out loud. "Yeah right. If not, then you're about the only woman in Summer Lake who hasn't. You get your very own silver fox."

Nina's smile disappeared. "I …" It was one thing to go out on a date up in Stanton Falls. That was different. Abbie wasn't there, none of her friends were. But here …?

Abbie squeezed her hand. "I'm only messing with you, Mom. But if you get the chance, you go for it, you hear me?"

Nina stared at her. Abbie had idolized her dad. Since he died, Nina had hidden so much from her in an attempt to help her hang onto her memories of who he'd been. Or at least, who she'd believed he was. She'd had it in her head that Abbie would struggle with it if she ever met someone else. Yet here she was encouraging her.

"Don't look like that. Life goes on if you give it the chance to. Dad wouldn't want you to become some sad old widow, would he? He'd want you to be happy again. You're not that old, you know."

Nina laughed at that last part. "I'm not that old at all, thank you."

Abbie laughed with her. "I know. You're young enough to meet someone new and make the most of it. You never know, Manny might be just the summer fling you need."

Nina shook her head slowly. She couldn't think about him that way.

Abbie raised her eyebrows. "Are you telling me you wouldn't be interested?"

"I don't think it's something I need to even think about, Abbs. You said yourself, he's a good-looking man and there are lots of women who think so. Even if he were looking for some kind of summer fling, I doubt I'd be his choice."

Chapter Five

Diego grasped Manny's shoulder as he walked him out to his car. "So, we'll see you at the Boathouse later?"

"Yeah. What time?"

"You tell me. Do you want to eat there? We can have dinner if you like?"

"Sure. You ask Izzy what time suits her and let me know." Manny was relieved. He'd been wondering whether he should just take himself out for dinner before meeting up with them anyway.

Diego laughed. "Let me guess; you're not looking forward to cooking for yourself?"

Manny pursed his lips. He'd had a great afternoon with Diego and his fiancée Izzy. They'd had a lot of catching up to do. The subject of where he was staying hadn't come up and he hadn't wanted to mention the way things had worked out with Nina and the house.

Diego raised an eyebrow and tightened his grip on Manny's shoulder. "What is it? What's wrong?"

"Nothing."

"Sorry, *mi amigo*, but your poker face just failed you. Something's up. Tell me?"

Manny let out a self-conscious chuckle. "There's nothing wrong. Nothing bad. It's just … well … you know the house I'm renting?"

Diego nodded.

"Do you know the woman who owns it?"

"Nina? She's Abbie's mom, no? I don't know her, but I've heard mention of her. Why?"

"Well …" Manny wondered if he should drop the subject. But the way Diego was watching his face expectantly told him there was no point even trying. If he didn't mention it now, it'd no doubt come out at some point. And then Diego would question why he'd been secretive. He blew out a sigh.

Diego chuckled. "Just tell me."

"Okay. Okay. I'm supposed to be renting the place from her. And—thanks to you—I'm here a few days earlier than she was expecting. She's here, too."

Diego's lips quirked up into a smile. "And?"

He had to laugh. "And last night—since I didn't know she was here and she didn't know I was—I grabbed her in her kitchen, thinking that she was an intruder."

Diego laughed. "And judging by the look on your face you wouldn't mind grabbing her again?"

Manny shook his head. "Trust you to jump to that conclusion."

"Am I wrong?"

Manny laughed. "I'm not answering that."

"So, I'm right."

"That isn't the point. The point is that she's back here and needs to stay at her house."

"So? You can stay with us or find another place."

"I don't need to."

Diego grinned. "You're going to stay with her? You work fast."

"We agreed that I would stay at the house—rent a room from her rather than the whole place."

"So, you're going to be roommates?"

"Yeah. I guess that's it."

"That's good, no?"

"Yeah. It is."

"You're not comfortable with it?"

"Not yet." He met Diego's gaze. "She's an attractive woman."

Diego laughed. "So, share her bed as well as her house."

Manny let out an exasperated laugh. "I should have known better than to try talking to you about it."

"What's the problem?"

"There is no problem. I'm not yet comfortable with how it will work, that's all. Anyway, we only got into this because I'd love to have dinner with you guys. I didn't know about going back to her house and eating there, or if she'd be eating there or how any of this is going to work."

Diego nodded. "Okay. I shall be good. I shall behave. Tonight, we'll have dinner at the Boathouse." He grinned. "And we'll work on your strategy for what happens next."

"I don't need a strategy. Nothing's going to happen."

Diego smirked. "Whatever you say, mi amigo. Whatever you say."

~ ~ ~

"Hey, you're early." Teresa opened the door and greeted Nina with a smile.

"Sorry. I wanted to get out of the house."

Teresa laughed. "Come on in. You do realize that you might be the only woman in town who doesn't want to make the most of every minute she can get with Manny Alvarado?"

Nina rolled her eyes. "It's one thing to daydream about. It's another when the man is right there in your house."

"I suppose. But I wouldn't mind finding out."

"If you're interested, I'll introduce you."

"Thanks, but I have a feeling about you and him. I wouldn't want to get in the way of that."

"There's nothing to get in the way of. And there won't be. He's renting a room from me and that's the only interest he has in me."

"But not the only interest you have in him?" Teresa arched an eyebrow.

"I'm not blind! He's a good-looking man. But be serious, Teresa. I'm a dowdy old widow. He could have his pick of any of the girls, even the girls Abbie's age."

Teresa shook her head. "If I've told you once I've told you a thousand times. You are a very attractive woman. Paul did a number on you. I wish you could get past that somehow. I wish you could see yourself as you are—as other people see you."

Nina didn't want to go where this conversation would inevitably take them. She dug in her purse and held up a bottle of wine. "I thought we could have a drink before we go."

Teresa gave her a stern look, but she let it go. "Great. Come on through to the kitchen. Did you get everything done that you needed to today?"

"I did. I caught up with Ben, and he's going to give me all the hours he can. And I had lunch with Abbie, and she's good with everything."

"Everything?"

"Yeah. She was a bit surprised about this house share situation, but she likes Manny, and if I'm going to have someone in the house, he's not a bad someone."

Teresa waggled her eyebrows.

"You know what I mean!" Nina couldn't help laughing.

"I do. You couldn't ask for better than your own, very sexy, special agent to protect you. And speaking of protecting you, did you tell Abbie about Brian?"

Nina dropped her gaze.

"I knew you wouldn't."

"There's no point. It's over with. It's not as though I'm still up there. I think I'd have to tell her if I were. But honestly, Teresa, I don't think I'm going to go back. I don't want to. I'm just going to have to find something here, so that I can stay."

"I like the sound of that. Selfishly, I'd love it if you come back, and from a practical point of view, you have the house and everything."

"I do." Nina wasn't sure that she wanted to keep it. But she didn't want to bring that up now. It'd only take them into another conversation she didn't want to have. Tonight was supposed to be a fun girl's night out.

She pulled up a seat at the island and raised her glass to her friend.

Teresa chinked hers against it. "What are we drinking to?"

Nina shrugged. "I don't even know."

Teresa grinned. "How about we just drink to good things— whatever they may be?"

"I like that. Good things." Nina sipped her wine. She could use some good things in her life.

It was almost nine by the time they made it to the Boathouse. Despite Nina's offer to treat her, they'd had dinner at Teresa's and then walked over there. It was a beautiful evening and it wasn't far.

Teresa slipped her arm through Nina's as they crossed the square. "If Manny's here, don't you worry about me, okay? I'm a big girl. I can see myself home."

Nina laughed. "Even if he is here, what difference would it make?"

"We'll have to wait and see, won't we?"

Nina shook her head. "There's nothing to see." She was surprised at the way the butterflies swirled in her stomach when she opened the door to the restaurant and stepped inside. Manny probably would be here. He'd said he was going out this evening, and it wasn't as though there were many places to go in Summer Lake on a Saturday night. But even if they ran into him … Even if he wanted to talk … She gave herself a shake. Teresa was getting inside her head, making her wonder what might happen. But that was crazy talk. Nothing was going to happen. Even if she wanted it to. Even if he was interested. Nothing could happen between them because … she frowned as she realized that there was no reason why not, no reason at all.

Manny scanned the room from his vantage point at the bar. He'd enjoyed dinner with Diego and Ted and their ladies, Izzy and Audrey. It was strange to him to see the two men he'd known for so many years in this new life that they'd built for themselves. He'd known them through his work for almost three decades. They'd lived through some tough situations together.

Now, they didn't exactly consider themselves retired—they still went back to the office in Laguna Beach occasionally, but they were living a very different life. They were here, with their women, hanging out with their families. Manny shook his head. Doing all the things a guy was supposed to do in retirement—all the things that he wouldn't be doing. He didn't have a family; he didn't have a woman.

"What can I get you, sugar?"

He smiled at the bartender, Kenzie. She was quite a character. "Another round for the table, if you will."

She smiled. "Sure thing. You can go and sit back down if you like. Your server can bring them over."

"That's okay. I'll take them."

"What's up? You need a minute away from the coupledom?"

He chuckled. "Maybe." It felt as though she'd read his mind. He was having fun with them all, but he was acutely aware that he was the lone single amongst them.

Kenzie grinned at him as she poured the drinks. "You know, they say if you can't beat 'em, join 'em? There are plenty of women here tonight who wouldn't mind helping you even up the numbers."

Manny shook his head. "I'm not looking."

She looked disappointed. "You're not? How come?"

He frowned. He hadn't asked himself that question yet. When he'd considered his retirement and what it would mean—what he was going to do with the rest of his life—he'd considered many aspects like where he would live, what he would do. He'd automatically seen the life he would build as a single life because he wasn't looking for a woman, but he hadn't stopped to question why not.

Kenzie held his gaze until he shrugged and said, "Honestly? I don't know."

She smiled. "From what I hear you just retired, right? You're thinking about moving up here, thinking about changing up your life. Why not consider something that might change everything?"

He looked back at her for a few moments then nodded. "Why not indeed."

Kenzie grinned. "Like I said, there are plenty of women here who'd love to hear that you're on the lookout."

He smiled. He was used to that. He didn't have a woman in his life. There hadn't been anyone long-term since his divorce. But he was aware of the effect he had on women. They liked him—they liked his looks at least, but that didn't count for much when it came down to spending anything more than a night together. He didn't think that sort of connection was something he should be looking for up here though. It was a small town; he knew how they worked. If he were to spend the night with a woman, it would only be if he had an eye on something more.

Just as he thought about what something more with a woman might look like at this point in his life, he spotted her. Nina. She was beautiful. His body knew it, he felt his heart rate pick up and the interest stir in his pants. To his surprise, though, his reaction wasn't just physical. Something in his mind switched when he saw her. He remembered the way she'd looked when she'd told him about that guy, Brian, and he wanted to go to her, wanted to protect her. He tried to tell himself that that was just what he did—who he was. Since he was a kid, he'd had strong protective instincts. He'd always looked out for his sisters and for smaller, weaker kids. His career had only honed and drawn upon those instincts for the last thirty years.

Kenzie set the tray of drinks in front of him and touched his arm. "Would I be right in guessing that all those women are going to be disappointed?"

He turned to meet her gaze.

"You're not on the lookout. You've already seen what you want. Right?"

He cocked his head to one side. He didn't want to answer. Even though he had the feeling she was right.

"Nina! Teresa!"

He closed his eyes when Kenzie called her and her friend over. She winked at him as they reached the bar.

"It's good to see you out, ladies. It's been a while. What can I get you? This one's on me."

"Hi, Kenzie. Thanks, sweetie, but you don't need to do that. I can—" Nina stopped mid-sentence when he turned, and she realized who he was.

He smiled. "I can get them. Please. It'd be my pleasure."

He didn't miss the way her cheeks colored up. He'd have to observe her some more to be sure, but he kind of already knew that he was the one who made her blush.

Her friend greeted him with a warm smile. "That's mighty nice of you." She stuck her hand out to shake with him. "I'm Teresa. Nina's best friend."

He smiled back as he shook with her. "It's nice to meet you."

"What'll it be ladies?" Kenzie grinned at them. "The usual?"

They both nodded.

Manny knew he should take the drinks to the table. The others would be waiting for them by now, but he didn't want to leave the bar now that Nina was here. He'd have to though. "I'll be right back, ladies."

He took the tray and hurried over to the table.

Diego looked up at him as he set the drinks down. "I was about to send out a search party."

Manny laughed. "No need. I just got talking at the bar."

Diego raised an eyebrow at him, but Izzy rolled her eyes and pushed at his arm. "You leave him alone." She winked at Manny.

Manny liked her a lot. He hadn't thought Diego would ever meet a woman who could keep up with him let alone tame him, but he'd surely met his match in Izzy.

Ted grinned at him. "Am I right in thinking that you're going back to the bar?"

Manny glanced over at where Nina and her friend where talking to Kenzie. "You are."

Ted nodded happily. "We'll see you later."

"Or not," added Diego as he walked away.

~ ~ ~

Teresa nudged Nina with her elbow. "He's coming back! I'm going to make myself scarce."

"Don't you dare. This is our first night out in months. I don't want you disappearing on me."

Teresa made a face. "But … Manny!"

Nina laughed. "But nothing. Promise you won't go home without me?"

Teresa sighed. "I promise. But I really have to go to the ladies' room." She giggled and set her drink down, walking away at the last possible moment so that Nina couldn't say anything to stop her without Manny overhearing it.

He smiled when he reached her. It made her heart race. He had a great smile. And his eyes! They were beautiful, big and brown like pools of melted chocolate. There was something about them, not just about the way they looked, more about the way they looked at her. There was kindness in his eyes. That was it. It was a strange thing to think, but it was true. He had the kindest eyes she'd ever seen. That didn't necessarily go with the rest of him. The rest of him looked big and tough. Hard even. There was no softness about him, even his face looked as though it could have been carved from granite, but there was such gentleness in his eyes.

She caught herself, realizing that she was sitting there staring into his eyes like an idiot. What must he think?

"Thanks for the drinks." It sounded stupid. But she had to say something and that was all she could think of.

He smiled. "It's my pleasure. I was hoping you'd be here tonight."

Her heart thundered in her chest. "You were?"

He nodded. "I didn't like to ask what your plans were. It felt too … intrusive. But now, here, we're in a more neutral environment."

She nodded, not sure she understood what he meant.

He perched on the stool beside her then looked confused.

"What's wrong?" she asked.

He laughed. "I need to get another drink. I took mine over to the guys and left it with them." He met her gaze for a moment. "It seems you throw me off."

She swallowed. Hard. He threw her off, too, but she wasn't sure she should tell him so.

She was relieved when Kenzie broke the moment. She set a drink down in front of him with a smile. "Here you go, sugar."

He picked up the glass and raised it to Nina.

She raised hers and waited.

He chuckled. "I don't know what to say we're drinking to."

She smiled. "Teresa and I figured it out earlier." She raised her glass a little higher. "To good things."

When he smiled back at her, it felt like a very good thing.

Chapter Six

Manny leaned against the pillar as he watched Nina dance with her friend, Teresa. He enjoyed watching her—watching her dance, watching her chat with her friends, watching her walk across the room. Anything. It didn't matter what. She was beautiful, but there was something more than that. He couldn't name what the something more was, but there was no denying that it existed.

He smiled through pursed lips when Diego's hand came down on his shoulder.

"You really think you can sneak up on me?"

Diego laughed. "I was hoping. I mean, you are somewhat distracted right now, no?"

He nodded but didn't say anything. There was no point in trying to pretend that he hadn't taken his eyes off Nina all night.

"Are you sure you don't want to come and stay at our place?"

Manny raised an eyebrow.

"It seems to me that you want to get to know her better. Do you want to do that while you're staying under her roof?"

Manny rubbed his chin as he thought about it. "Yes. I believe I do."

"Okay then. I just wanted to give you an option."

"Thanks. I appreciate it."

Izzy came to stand between them and slipped one arm through Diego's and the other through Manny's. "What are we talking about, kiddies?"

Manny smiled. He liked Izzy. She was a good match for his friend. Better than he'd have thought possible.

"How well do you know Nina?" asked Diego.

"I don't really. I know Teresa a little bit, but Nina's been living up in Stanton Falls. I know her daughter, Abbie. She and her fiancé Ivan are friends with Zack."

Diego nodded. "That's right."

Izzy waggled her eyebrows at Manny. "Are you interested?"

He smiled. She was about as subtle as Diego. "I'm staying at her house."

Izzy frowned. "Oh. That's right. But she's back in town? How's that going to work?"

Diego chuckled. "That's what we're trying to figure out."

"There's nothing to figure out," said Manny. "Now that she's back I'm just renting a room from her instead of the whole house."

Izzy grinned at him. "If there's nothing to figure out, how come you're standing here watching her dance?"

He chuckled and looked at Diego. "You two are a pair together, no?"

Diego nodded happily and slung his arm around Izzy's shoulders. "We are. And that means we both want to see you happy, and we'd both love it if you chose to stay here. Especially if you stay because you met your special someone."

Manny shrugged.

"We should dance." Diego grinned at him, but he shook his head and looked up at the stage where Clay McAdam was singing some old country song.

"I like to listen, but I wouldn't know how to dance to this."

Diego laughed. "It's simple. You just grab your woman and shuffle your feet."

Izzy rolled her eyes as he wrapped her up in his arms and moved her slowly to the music. "You could ask Nina if she wants to dance?"

"No."

Diego grinned at him. "Not to this country music. But next time … next time we need to get the boys to play our music."

Manny couldn't help but chuckle at that.

Izzy gave them both a puzzled look. "Your music?"

"You still haven't discovered all my talents, mi amor. Manny and me? We grew up in Colombia. We love to dance."

"Salsa?" asked Izzy.

"Amongst other things," said Manny.

She clapped her hands together. "Oh, I have to hold you to this. This I need to see."

Diego grinned at Manny. "We'll be happy to show off for you, won't we?"

Manny allowed himself to watch Nina for a few moments as he nodded his agreement.

She turned and met his gaze just as the song came to an end. Teresa noticed and started making her way toward them.

Manny had to wonder if they could make it any more obvious when Izzy and Diego both started talking to Teresa and left Nina standing in front of him.

"Are you having a good evening?"

She smiled. "We are thanks. How about you? It must be good to catch up with your old friends."

"It is. It's been too long."

Diego turned and grinned at them. "Catching up with old friends is overrated. It's more important to make new friends."

Manny shot him a dark look. It was typical Diego to be so over the top. There was no rush. He didn't want Nina to feel under any pressure. He didn't want to feel any himself.

Diego put an arm around Izzy's shoulders and another around Teresa's. As he started leading them away, Teresa turned back and gave Nina a meaningful look.

Manny blew out a sigh. "I'm sorry."

To his relief, she laughed. "I'm sorry, too. It seems that your friends are as bad as mine."

He glanced back at Teresa who was now standing at the bar with Diego and Izzy. She grinned and nodded at him, making him chuckle. "It would seem so. I thought perhaps your friend was not so approving."

He loved the sound of her laugh. It was a little raspy, as though it didn't get that much use. "Oh, she approves. A little too forcefully."

"And as you noticed, Diego and Izzy do, too. Do you mind?"

She looked up at him, and there was a vulnerability about her that made him want to close his arms around her. "Mind?" she asked.

"That our friends have left you in a situation where you seem to be stuck with me, and there's no one to rescue you if you need it."

The way she smiled made his heart race. "I don't see it as being stuck with you—and I can't think of anyone I'd rather have come to my rescue if I need it."

He held her gaze for a long moment, wanting nothing more than to put his arm around her and take her out of here, take her somewhere they could talk and get to know each other better.

Her smile faded. "Sorry. I shouldn't have said that, should I? I'm sure you're sick of women wanting you to rescue them."

He couldn't resist sliding his arm around her waist as he started walking her toward the doors. "I haven't paid any attention to what women want in a long time. I'd be happy to rescue you if you need it, and I get the feeling ..." He stopped and looked down into her eyes "That you might be the one to rescue me."

Nina's heart felt as though it might beat right out of her chest as they walked out of the restaurant onto the back deck. She didn't know what had possessed her to say what she had—about him being the man she'd want to come to her rescue.

She didn't know why she'd said it, but she had even less clue why Manny had responded the way he had—that she might be the one to rescue him? What did that even mean?

The cool night air fanned her cheeks as they walked across the deck. She finally stopped when they reached the railing over the water and there was nowhere else to go.

Manny rested his elbow on the railing and looked down into her eyes, making her heart race again.

She searched his face. He was an imposing figure, there was no question about that. He was tall, over six feet she'd guess.

His shoulders were broad, his arms muscular. In fact, everything about him was muscular. His face was hard, until he smiled. He smiled now, and ... damn. It didn't just soften his face, it softened her knees and possibly every muscle in her body, too. She leaned on the railing to support herself.

"I told you, you throw me. I'm sorry. I'm blowing this, aren't I?"

"Blowing what?" She thought she knew what he was saying, but she couldn't believe that was what he meant.

He met her gaze, as if checking that she was being honest with him. That she really didn't understand what he meant. He nodded as if convinced that she was genuine, not just toying with him.

"Blowing my chance at getting to know you." He raised an eyebrow.

She shook her head slowly.

"I'm sorry." He spoke quickly. His voice sounding much harsher than before. He looked almost scary, the furrows in his brow making a formidable scowl.

She rested her hand on his arm. Her intention was to reassure him, but that slight touch had an effect neither of them could deny—or knew what to do with. She'd felt the same shock race up her arm this morning when their hands had brushed against each other mopping up the spilled water. She'd thought then that it was nerves. Now, she knew better. It was him, Manny, and the effect he had on her. And judging from the expression on his face, she had the same effect on him.

She smiled and loved the way his expression softened in response. "I wasn't saying no. You're *not* blowing it. I don't think either of us is doing a good job with this, but ... I'd like to get to know you, too."

A wave of heat rushed through her when he rested his hand on top of hers. "Thank you. And now that we have that out in the open, perhaps we can slow down?"

It was her turn to frown.

He squeezed her hand. "Forgive me. I don't want to rush you; I don't want to rush myself. We've been honest with each other that there's an interest. Why don't we see where it takes us?" He smiled again. "I'm here for the next month at least. There's no question that we'll be seeing a lot of each other."

She had to smile at that. Of course, they would. He was staying in her house. She nodded. "Thank you. I don't know where I want things to go ... I don't know ..." What she didn't know was what to say. Paul had been gone for two years. At first, she hadn't thought that she'd ever want to be with another man. It was only a few weeks since she'd gone on the first date she'd ever been on with someone who wasn't him. And that hadn't exactly turned out well. She shook her head, hoping that he might somehow understand.

It seemed that he did. "We don't need to know anything more than we already do. We know that there's an interest we'd like to explore." His eyes twinkled when he smiled, and it set the butterflies swirling in her stomach.

"Would you like another drink?" he asked.

"Okay."

As they walked back inside, Manny placed his hand in the small of her back. He'd almost reached for her hand; that seemed like the natural thing to do, but perhaps it wasn't the wisest. He was more used to being the observer than the observed, in any situation. He knew that anyone observing them might see his hand on her back as something any guy would do to guide a woman through a crowded place, but hand holding? That would tell a different story.

She looked up at him when they reached the bar. "What would you like? I'll get them."

He frowned. He planned to get their drinks. That was what a man did, as far as he was concerned.

To his surprise, she laughed. "Don't look at me like that. You're not going to be able to boss me around by giving me stern looks."

He chuckled. "Sorry. I suppose that's a habit I'm going to have to unlearn."

She raised an eyebrow in question.

"I'm used to working with a team. I'm used to letting them know what I expect without having to say a word."

She smiled. "I understood what you meant. You thought you should get the drinks." She shrugged. "But I'm saying I'm getting them." She met his gaze with what looked like a challenge in her eyes. "Is that a problem?"

"No problem at all. I'll have a whisky, thanks."

He let out a sigh when he saw Diego coming to join them. No matter what Nina might think about buying the drinks, he knew that Diego would have a different opinion. Where they came from it was the guy's job.

To his relief, Izzy and Teresa appeared at his side, and Izzy spoke before Diego had the chance to chide him for what he would no doubt perceive as his lack of chivalry.

"Nina. It's lovely to meet you properly. Teresa tells me you're back to stay?"

Manny watched her expression. He'd guess that she wasn't entirely sure that she was here to stay, and that she wished her friend hadn't said she was. She covered it up with a friendly smile which he was sure was all that anyone else would notice.

"I think so. Things changed up in Stanton. There wasn't enough work for all of us, so I'm back for now, at least."

"Well, I hope you'll stick around. I haven't been here for long and I'm starting to get to know everyone. It seems like there's quite a group of us giving life a second chance in Summer Lake."

Manny pursed his lips. It was true that Izzy and Ted's fiancée, Audrey, were giving life a second chance here as she put it. He had to wonder if Nina would see it that way, though. Her life was different now because her husband had died. Not because she'd moved here to start a new chapter. He needn't have worried.

Nina smiled. "So I hear. We should all get together for lunch or something. We should get some of the girls who've lived here forever together with you newbies. Summer Lake isn't the kind of place where you get cliques of newcomers versus old-timers, but it could turn that way if we don't all make the effort."

Izzy nodded happily. "You'll have to give me your number and we'll set something up."

Diego smiled at him over the top of the girls' heads, and he had to smile back.

Teresa set her glass down on the bar and yawned. "Make sure you include me when you set things up, won't you? I'm pooped. I'm going to head home."

Manny got the impression that she was deliberately making herself scarce—that she found herself in the same position that he'd been in earlier; the only single with two couples. He glanced at Nina. They were hardly a couple, but that was the way it felt.

"Just let me finish this," said Nina.

Teresa shot Manny a conspiratorial smile before she answered Nina. "That's okay. You stay."

Manny's heart beat faster as he wondered what she would say. She glanced at him but then shook her head. "Nope. You promised me you wouldn't go home without me."

Teresa frowned at her. "I'm fine. It's a five-minute walk."

Manny could tell from the look on her face that Nina wasn't going to let her friend leave by herself. He liked her for it, though he hated to think that she was probably paranoid about a woman walking home alone after what had happened to her in Stanton Falls.

He downed his whisky and smiled at them. "I'm ready to call it a night myself. Why don't we all go?"

Nina, Teresa, Diego, and Izzy all smiled at him. And although they each had different reasons for doing so, it made him happy that they all liked his suggestion.

~ ~ ~

When they reached the corner of Teresa's street, Nina hugged her. "Thanks for tonight. I'll give you a call tomorrow."

Teresa grinned at her and nodded, with a look that said, *if you don't call me, I'll call you.* "Thanks for coming out. It's so good to have you back."

"It's good to be back."

Teresa turned to Manny, and he leaned down to peck her cheek. "It was a pleasure to meet you."

Teresa laughed. "You too, but don't go sounding so formal. You're going to be seeing a lot more of me, and I don't do formal."

Nina laughed. "She's right. You might as well get used to us."

"And in that case," added Teresa, "you should know that I'm a hugger."

Nina wanted to laugh again at the expression on Manny's face when Teresa wrapped him in a hug. She was glad to see him relax and hug her back.

"You can probably tell that I'm not much of a hugger," he said with a smile. "At least, I haven't been, but I could learn."

"You stick with us," said Teresa. "You'll learn fast. Anyway …" She opened her front gate. "Thanks for tonight. This was fun."

They watched her open her front door and go inside before they walked on. Nina's heart started to race again. She hadn't walked home with a guy after a night out since she was a teenager. She sneaked a glance at Manny; of course, he caught her and smiled.

Her heart pounded even harder when he held his hand out to her. She looked down at it and then up into his eyes. What she saw in them made her smile and take his hand.

"Is that okay?" he asked.

"It's nice."

He squeezed her hand. "Are you a hugger, too?"

"I am. I always have been."

He smiled. "Maybe you can teach me."

She sucked in a deep breath and nodded. She'd be happy to.

They reached the house just a few minutes later and she dug in her purse for her keys. While she was searching, Manny held his up.

"Is it okay?"

She nodded. It felt strange to watch him open her front door and let them into her house—the house that she and Paul had shared for most of her life. It felt strange, but it didn't feel bad. He turned on the light in the hallway and a memory flashed before her eyes. She saw Paul standing there, his face twisted in contempt. That was one of the last times she'd seen him. The last time he'd been in the house. She closed her eyes willing the memory away. When she opened them again it was gone. Manny stood there his eyes filled with concern.

"Are you all right? Is it … wrong … me being here?"

She gave him a weak smile. "It's … strange. Not wrong."

"Are you sure?"

She nodded. "I am. Thanks for checking, though."

He held her gaze for a long moment and she felt as though he could see everything. As though somehow, he knew the truth, even though she'd hidden that from everyone—even from her own daughter.

He stepped toward her and her heart started to race. Not in a good way this time. She wasn't ready. It wouldn't feel right. She couldn't …

To her relief, he stopped and held his arms out to his sides. "Like I said. I'm in no hurry. I think the best thing for me to do tonight is go to my room." He smiled that smile that made his eyes seem so gentle. "Is there any chance I could get some hugging practice before I go?"

How could a guy who looked so tough be so sweet? She nodded and stepped toward him, wrapping her arms around his shoulders in what she intended to be a friendly hug.

When his arms closed around her, she closed her eyes. She had no choice. She felt as though all the stress and tension left her body and her mind. She rested her head against his shoulder and breathed him in. His arms tightened around her and he dropped a kiss on top of her head before stepping away from her with a smile.

She felt lost and alone, cold where his arms had been warm. And that was ridiculous! She'd known the man for less than twenty-four hours, and she had no right to be hugging on him at all—let alone wondering about more.

He held her gaze for a long moment. "You might make a hugger out of me yet."

She chuckled. "I'd be happy to try."

"It'd take lots of practice. I have a lifetime's worth of prickliness to overcome."

"I don't see you as prickly."

He chuckled. "That's because you bring out the best in me. I assure you, though, I'll need a lot of practice."

She smiled. "I'll be happy to help." She couldn't resist. She put her hands on his shoulders and stood on her tiptoes to plant a kiss on his cheek. "Goodnight, Manny."

When his arms closed around her again, she closed her eyes and hoped for more. He landed another kiss on top of her head, and breathed, "Goodnight, Nina." Then he was gone.

She was cold and alone again standing in the hallway watching him disappear up the stairs.

She sucked in a deep breath and exhaled slowly, glad that he'd had the sense to go before she asked him not to.

Chapter Seven

Manny opened his eyes and lay staring at the ceiling for a few minutes. It wasn't too far out of the ordinary for him to wake up on a Sunday morning and have no plans for the day. He could handle that. What was throwing him was the realization that tomorrow would be Monday, and he wouldn't have any plans then either. He wouldn't need to roll out of bed and head out for a run. Wouldn't need to take a quick shower before hurrying to the office. He wasn't sure how he felt about that. It was probably better not to examine it too closely yet. He'd deal with tomorrow when it arrived.

He smiled and swung his legs out of bed. Today was already here. He might not have any plans, but he was hoping that was a good thing. He was hoping that Nina might not have any plans either and that maybe they'd do something together.

He opened the bedroom door quietly and listened. The house was quiet. He'd guess that she wasn't up yet. He made his way downstairs silently. He'd already figured out which stairs creaked and where to step to make no noise.

The kitchen was bright and airy; the early morning sun shone through the windows making him smile. He reached for the carafe and filled it with water. Nina had said that she needed the first cup of coffee in the morning to settle her down. He was the same way, and he hoped that having it ready for when she came down would make her smile.

Once it was brewing, he went to the back door and opened it. The yard was small, but it had everything you could need. There was a patio area with a table and chairs and a grill that looked old but serviceable. Maybe she'd let him make her dinner out here one night.

He turned at the sound of her coming downstairs and smiled when she came into the kitchen. She didn't look as though she'd just woken up. She looked as though she'd showered and gotten dressed and ready before she came down. It made him sad to realize that she wasn't relaxed in her own home— because of him.

"Good morning."

"Good morning." He smiled and pointed to the coffee pot. "It's almost ready, and I think I made it the way you like it—as strong as yesterday."

The way she smiled made him feel as though he'd slayed dragons for her. "Oh, my goodness! Thank you. If you're going to make me coffee every morning, I might never let you leave!"

He chuckled. "That's good to know."

Her cheeks flushed pink. "Sorry. You know what I mean."

"It's okay. I do." He wanted to say something more, wanted to tell her he'd be happy to make her coffee every morning, but it was better to let it go. She was embarrassed enough.

He reached for a mug and then stopped. "Sorry. I was about to pour it, but I think we maybe need to establish some ground rules."

She gave him a puzzled look. "About pouring coffee?"

He laughed. "No. About us sharing space. I don't want to overstep. To me, it's not unusual to be in a rental property. I have to set up base wherever I'm working. I make myself at home. But this is your home. I don't want to come in and take over."

She smiled. "Thanks. I hadn't even thought about that. I suppose, if anything I was thinking that I should be taking care of you … you know, you're a guest in my house."

"I don't think I like that idea. I don't want to be a burden, don't want to create work for you."

"It's not a burden. I like it."

She meant it. She was one of those women who took care of the people around her, he could tell.

She laughed. "We'll figure it out. But first, coffee."

He chuckled. "And since I'm closest, I'll pour." He handed her a mug and watched her add cream and sugar.

She sat down at the counter and took a few sips before looking up at him. "Now I'm on the way to feeling human again."

He smiled and drank his coffee in silence. He didn't need the caffeine as badly as Nina seemed to, but he did enjoy this quiet ritual in the morning. He was surprised that it was still as enjoyable, if not more so in her company. She didn't speak. He didn't feel the need to. He wasn't sure that he'd ever shared companionable silence with a woman before. He smiled again when he realized that he wouldn't have believed it was possible.

When Manny went back upstairs to take a shower, Nina took her second cup of coffee out into the back yard. She sat down at the patio table and closed her eyes as the sun warmed her face. It was going to be a hot day.

She opened her eyes again and blew out a sigh as she looked around the yard. It'd be a perfect day for a swim. She'd always wanted a pool. The yard wasn't that big, but there'd be room for a pool. Years ago, Paul had agreed that they could have one. She'd gotten quotes from a couple local companies and they hadn't been as much as she'd expected. She'd been thrilled. But Paul had turned cold on the idea. He'd decided that it would be better to save the money for their retirement.

She took a big gulp of her coffee. At least, that's what he'd said. She knew better now. Now, of course, she knew that he wouldn't live long enough to retire. She swallowed around the lump in her throat and blinked away the tears. She also knew that he hadn't wanted to save the money at all. He'd had other things to spend it on.

She made a face when she heard her phone ringing in the kitchen. It'd probably be Teresa wanting to talk about last night. She hurried inside to get it before it stopped ringing.

She smiled when she saw Abbie's name on the display. "Good morning, love," she answered. "You're up early."

Abbie laughed. "Yeah, but not by choice. You know me better than that. Ivan went out for a run before it gets too hot and I couldn't get back to sleep. I thought it'd be a good time to catch up with you. How are things? How's Manny? I should warn you that you might as well tell me everything. Most of the gang weren't at the Boathouse last night, but I told Kenzie she had to keep an eye on you."

Nina had to laugh. "Why would she need to keep an eye on me?" Even as she asked, she glanced upstairs at the sound of Manny moving around and decided to go back outside.

"Err, I think you know full well why, young lady."

She laughed again remembering all the times she'd said those exact words to Abbie when she was younger. "I should do what you used to do and play dumb, pretend I don't know what you're talking about."

Abbie laughed with her. "Sorry. I can see now how stupid that was. You must have hated me."

"I could never hate you, Abbs. I love you more than anything in the world. I always have. You frustrated the heck out of me back then, but you were a kid. And I'm not a kid." She smiled to herself. "So, I don't have to tell you a thing."

"No, you don't. You're right. I'm sorry."

She laughed. "I don't have to tell you anything, but I want to. So, ask away."

"I want to know all about Manny, obviously! I want to know if you're really going to share your house with him for the next month. And if ... you know ... if there's anything going on between you ... or if you think there might be."

Nina pressed her lips together trying to keep in a smile.

"Mom!"

"What?"

"Say something! Your silence makes me think that there's already something going on."

"Would you mind if there was?"

Abbie was quiet for a moment before she answered. "I don't know. You know I think he's great, and I like the idea of you and him seeing each other ..."

"But?"

"But that's just the idea of it. When I think about it as reality ... and especially a reality that might have already happened ... when you've only known each other a couple of days ... I don't think I like that so much."

"Well, you've got nothing to worry about. It's not a reality ... and I'm not even going to ask what you think might have happened ... but there's something there, Abbs. I do like him. We even talked about it."

"About what? What did he say?"

Nina had to laugh. "I get the feeling that you're talking about sex." She glanced over her shoulder to make sure that she'd closed the patio door.

Abbie laughed with her. "Well, yeah, and no. I mean … ugh. I don't want to even think about it. But at the same time, it's hard not to. I don't want to think about someone taking advantage of you, but at the same time I get that you're still a woman. You should be able to if you want to and … I can see the appeal."

"Okay. Well, I'm glad we've cleared that up. That hasn't happened. And don't expect me to tell you about it if it ever does."

"I wouldn't! I don't! I just … All I meant was that I didn't like the idea that … you know … on a first date … I …"

"I know. He's not like that. And neither am I."

"Okay. Good. I'll be happy to move on from there. So, what did you guys talk about?"

"Well …" Nina glanced up at the house again. "We both admitted that there's an interest there, and that we'd like to see if anything develops from it."

"Aww. I like that."

Nina hugged her arm around herself and warmth spread through her chest. "I do, too."

"So, what are you guys going to do today?"

"I don't know. I don't have any plans. I don't know if he does, and I don't like to ask."

"Yeah, I guess that must be awkward. Well, I hope you two decide to do something together, but if he has other plans or if you want to get away, you know you're welcome over here. We're having a lazy day."

"Thanks, love. I don't think so. You and Ivan don't get many days off together. You don't need me around."

Abbie laughed. "It was Ivan's suggestion. You know he loves having you over. Plus, I think he wants to interrogate you about Manny. He's been interrogating everyone else since I told him about your house share situation."

Nina smiled. "Aww, tell him I said thank you. He's so good looking out for me. I'll bake him some cookies in the week. He's a good boy."

"I won't tell him that last bit. He's seeing himself as the big man—the man of the family who's not happy about this Manny guy being around his mother-in-law."

"Tell him I can take care of myself. And besides, Manny's a very good guy. He has nothing to worry about."

"You can tell him that yourself soon enough. If you don't come over today, you can expect a visit from us very soon. He wants to know that you're all right."

Nina turned to see Manny standing in the doorway holding up the coffee pot. She nodded at him and picked up her mug.

"Well, I'll see you soon, I'm sure."

"Oh! Is he there?"

She smiled as Manny gestured for her to stay seated and came to refill her mug. "Yes."

"Ooh. I'll leave you to it, then. Talk to you soon. Love you, Mom."

"Love you, too, Abbs."

She ended the call and smiled up at Manny. "Thanks."

"Sorry. I didn't mean to interrupt you."

"It's fine. It was Abbie. We were done anyway."

He nodded and turned to go back inside.

"Do you want to join me?"

He smiled at her over his shoulder. "I'd love to, if you're sure?"

"Yes. Abbie was just checking in while Ivan's out for his run." She got to her feet. "I can make some breakfast, if you're hungry?"

"Actually, I was wondering if …" He frowned. "Would you like to go out to eat? Ted told me that they do a great breakfast at the resort."

Nina pursed her lips. She knew that breakfast at the resort was a big thing for a lot of people in town. It was where everyone caught up with each other, and it was also a see-and-be-seen kind of thing. That wasn't her style. When Paul was still around, they rarely ate out, and since he'd been gone …

Manny raised an eyebrow. "Just a suggestion." The corners of his lips lifted up in the hint of a smile. "I understand if you don't want to be seen having breakfast with me."

She felt the heat in her cheeks. Boy, she wished she could stop herself from blushing so much around him! She let out an embarrassed laugh. "It's not that … well, maybe a little bit that, but it's more about seeing people and having to catch them all up on why I'm back and what's going on with me."

"Of course. No problem."

She followed him into the kitchen and added more cream and sugar to her coffee, wishing that she'd just said yes. "I'm sure you'll run into lots of people you know though. You won't have to eat alone."

That frown was back; if she didn't already know better, she'd be scared of that look.

He held her gaze for a moment and she felt a wave of goose bumps race down her arms. "I only suggested the Boathouse because I didn't want you to have to cook." His eyes softened when he smiled. "I seem to be blowing it again, but what I'm interested in is having breakfast with you—not where we have it."

She smiled back at him. "Okay, then. In that case, you should know that I love to cook. And I'm more of a homebody than the kind who likes to go out all the time. So, how does an omelet sound?"

He chuckled. "That sounds wonderful. Thank you."

"You get yourself comfortable then, and I'll get to it."

Manny sat on one of the stools at the counter and had to admire her ass when she bent to get a pan from the bottom cabinet.

When she straightened up, she looked surprised to see him there. "You can sit in the living room, if you like."

He couldn't help wondering if that was what she was used to—what she expected from a man—that he would lounge in the other room while she cooked for him.

He smiled. "I'm happy right here. I don't want to be the guest who you cook for. I want to hang out with you. Like … friends do."

She looked surprised, but pleasantly so. "Okay, then. Great."

He watched her crack eggs and move around the kitchen, obviously at ease in her environment, but then she would be. From what he understood, this had been her home for many years.

"Has Abbie always lived here?"

She shook her head without turning around. "No. She moved away straight after high school. Went down to the city with a boyfriend. She only came back when … after her father died."

"Oh. I'm sorry." He'd hoped to get to know more about her without having to ask about her husband.

She turned around and smiled. "Don't be. It's wonderful to have her back here. And it's turned out to be the best thing that ever happened to her. She has a great job now. She works at the medical center. And she's engaged to a wonderful guy, Ivan. I'm sure you'll meet him." She chuckled. "In fact, I should probably warn you that Abbie said he intends to check you out. He's not sure that he approves of our house sharing arrangement."

"Then I like him already."

She gave him a puzzled look.

"Honestly, if I were in his shoes, I wouldn't approve either. I wouldn't be happy if any of the women in my life were sharing their home with a stranger."

"Are there many women in your life?"

He had to hide his smile at the way she asked so quickly. It reassured him. "There are a few. My mom's been gone for many years. But I have two sisters and my ex-wife." He wondered what she'd make of that and liked her more when she smiled.

"You're still close with your ex-wife?"

"Yes. We're much better at being friends than we were at being married. Well, I am. She's good at being married now."

"Are you friends with her husband, too?"

He chuckled. "I've been friends with him since we were ten years old."

"Oh, wow!"

People were usually surprised when they learned that his ex-wife had married his best childhood friend—and that he couldn't be happier for them. He shrugged. "Kim and I should never have gotten married. We were young and ..." He shrugged again. "I was already married to my work. I didn't have enough left over to give to her. She wanted a family, she deserved that. And she deserved someone who wanted to put her first. It was sad when we split, but we both knew it was the right thing to do. Andrés had always been around. He was my best friend. He was one of our friends. After the divorce, he and Kim remained friends, and with time, they discovered that they were right for each other."

She gave him a puzzled look. "And that didn't bother you?"

He laughed. "Honestly, it didn't. We joke around, the three of us, that it should have been obvious all along. They were supposed to be the couple, I was supposed to be the friend."

She shook her head. "I can't imagine. I'm glad you all ended up happy, though."

He nodded. "I can't imagine what it would be like to have had a long and happy marriage." He hoped that might give her an opening to talk about hers.

Instead, she turned back to the stove.

"I'm sorry."

"You don't need to apologize all the time." She spoke without turning around.

She kind of had a point. He'd probably said he was sorry more in the last couple days than he had in the last several years. He smiled and stopped himself from apologizing again. "I'm out of my element here. I'm used to knowing what to say and knowing what to do. With you I feel like I keep getting it wrong, and the last thing I want to do is upset you."

She turned around and smiled. "You didn't upset me. I kind of upset myself. When you said you couldn't imagine what it was like to have a long and happy marriage, I almost agreed with you, almost admitted that I can't imagine that either."

He wanted to ask what she meant. He could no doubt get her to explain. But instead, he watched her face and waited for her to continue.

She met his gaze and shrugged. "There's something about you. I've managed to keep up the façade for people who I've known for years—even my own daughter. They all believe that I did have a long and happy marriage." He watched as she twisted the dishcloth in her hands. "It was long, but it was far from happy."

He didn't know what to say. Didn't know if she was looking for sympathy or simply finding relief in confessing the truth to a stranger.

"Anyway." She forced a smile. "I usually throw everything I can find in an omelet, but I don't have much in yet. Does ham and cheese sound okay?"

"That sounds great. Thanks."

As she turned back to the stove, he could see that her shoulders were shaking. Not enough to say that she was crying, but enough to signal her distress. He only thought about it for a moment before he slid down from the stool and went to her.

Knowing how easily she startled, he spoke before he put his hand on her shoulder. "Are you okay?"

She spun around her eyes wide in surprise. She nodded. Her eyes shone with tears, but she didn't allow them to fall. "I'm sorry. I don't know why I even told you that."

"Perhaps because you needed to get it off your chest and it's easier to talk to a stranger."

She looked up into his eyes, and what he saw in hers made his heart rate pick up. "You don't feel like a stranger."

He shook his head. "I don't want to be one." He couldn't help it. He slid his arm around her waist and slowly drew her toward him. "Do you think now might be a good time to give me another hugging lesson?"

He felt her nod against his chest when he closed his arms around her. The way she felt with her arms around him, the warmth and softness of her against his chest told him he didn't need lessons when it came to hugging her; it felt like the most natural thing in the world.

Chapter Eight

After breakfast, Nina started to rinse the dishes and load them into the dishwasher, but Manny came and took the plate from her hands. "Let me do them?"

She couldn't help smiling as she nodded. It was wonderful that he wanted to help out, but just being so close to him was what made her smile. She hoped her cheeks weren't red again, but she knew her heart was racing. It was just the effect he had on her.

When he'd hugged her earlier, the tears had soon dried up in her eyes. She'd gone from feeling sorry for herself and for the mess that her marriage had been to feeling something very different indeed. With Manny's arms around her, with her face buried in his hard chest, she'd felt … aroused.

She stepped away and watched him take care of the dishes. "Thank you."

He smiled over his shoulder at her. "It's the least I can do. You cooked for me. It's only fair that I should clean up afterward."

She nodded. She hadn't even been thanking him for cleaning up. But she could hardly tell him that. There was no way she'd tell him that she was thanking him for reminding her how it felt to be a woman.

When he'd loaded the machine and wiped down the countertops, he came to stand before her. Her heart rate picked up again. Butterflies took to flight in her stomach.

He cocked his head to one side. "Are you okay?"

She nodded mutely then closed her eyes when he put his hand on her shoulder. It took everything she had not to rest her cheek against it.

"What do you usually do on a Sunday?"

She stared at him blankly for a moment. She heard the question but couldn't focus on it. She was too distracted by the waves of heat his hand sent coursing through her.

He cocked his head to one side.

"I … err … I haven't been here on the weekends in a long time."

"Of course. It wasn't the right question anyway."

She gave him a puzzled look, and he smiled.

"What I really wanted to ask is what you'd like to do today and if you'd like to do it with me."

She bit down on her bottom lip. She wasn't going to answer honestly.

His eyes twinkled when he smiled, and she had to wonder if he'd read her mind somehow. "Sorry. That sounded wrong. I meant if you'd like to do something together."

She couldn't keep in the laugh that came out as a snort. "What kind of something did you have in mind?"

He laughed. "I'm making a mess of this again, aren't I? I'm not trying to proposition you, honestly."

"That's a shame." Her hand came up to cover her mouth as soon as the words were out. Then she had to laugh.

To her relief, he laughed with her. "You want to be careful. If you say things like that, I might have to proposition you, after all."

She looked up into his eyes. His hand was still on her shoulder. Her body was pretty much buzzing with the closeness of him. She couldn't make herself speak, so she just nodded.

His eyebrows came together in a trace of a frown, and his eyes bored into hers. "May I kiss you?"

Her heart leaped into her mouth as she nodded again. He lifted his hand from her shoulder to cup her cheek. Her heart felt as though it might beat right out of her chest as he stepped closer. She lifted her chin so that she could still look up into his eyes as his other arm slid around her waist.

"I told myself I wouldn't do this," he breathed.

She searched his face. "Why?"

"Because I thought I should take my time. Give you the chance to decide if it's what you want."

She couldn't tell him just how badly she wanted it. Instead, she simply nodded. "It is." She closed her eyes and waited. She should probably be more proactive about it, she knew that, but she wouldn't know how even if she wanted to, and in that moment, she didn't want to. His big strong arm felt so good around her. He made her feel safe, which was crazy after what had happened to her just the other night. Crazy as it might be, she trusted him.

He stroked his thumb across her cheek so gently. She opened her eyes only to find his inches away. Then he brushed his thumb over her lips, sending shivers racing down her spine. She couldn't help thinking that he was putting more thought and tenderness into a kiss than Paul had put into their lovemaking in years—maybe ever.

~ ~ ~

Manny held her gaze as he lowered his head. She was nervous, but not afraid. He'd thought she would be—that she should be. But all her responses were telling him loud and clear that she trusted him. He wasn't going to allow himself to acknowledge that they were also signaling that she wanted him. He couldn't go anywhere near that thought until she actually spoke the words.

Her lips were full and soft as he brushed his over them. He should leave it at that. He should pull back. There was no rush. She needed time and space—so did he. Her arms came up around his shoulders and drowned out the voice of reason. She pressed her lips against his and that was all it took. He held her closer to his chest and claimed her mouth in a kiss that would leave her in no doubt that he wanted her, too.

She clung to him as she kissed him back. Her tongue met his with an eagerness that surprised him. All the tension left her as she softened in his arms and pressed herself against him. He let himself get lost in her, but not completely. He'd exercised self-control in every aspect of his life for the last thirty-some years. Now that he'd finally found the woman he knew could make him lose control, he had to hold back for her sake.

When he finally lifted his head, her cheeks were flushed, and her eyes were shining. He had to ignore the way her chest rose and fell as she breathed slow and shallow.

"I didn't expect that."

Her eyes darted up to meet his. "I didn't either. Well, I thought … I thought it'd be good to kiss you … but …"

He had to smile. "Same here. I knew it would be good, but I didn't know that you'd blow me away."

"I did?" She looked thrilled.

He chuckled. "You did."

"Well, that's good to know. You blew me away, too. But then that's not hard. I don't have …"

He frowned when she stopped herself. "What don't you have?"

She shrugged and tightened her arms around his waist. "It doesn't matter. What matters is that we both liked it." She looked up at him with a smile. "And I hope that means that we'll get to kiss again … sometime."

He dropped a peck on her lips. "Oh, we will. Our first kiss will not be our last." He frowned as a thought occurred to him. It seemed too far-fetched to even consider.

"Are you sure about that?"

"I am. Sorry. I just had a thought."

"What?"

He smiled down at her. "I'm not going to tell you. Not yet. But I will write it down."

She watched as he went to the pad she kept by the telephone. This was a habit he'd gotten into at work. When an unbidden thought came to him about what the outcome of an investigation might be, but it was way too soon for it to be anything more than a hunch, he would write it down and put it in a sealed and dated envelope.

It had become a joke around the office that maybe they should be called the FBH—the Federal Bureau of Hunches—because there was no need for investigations. They only ever proved out Manny's hunches.

He smiled to himself as he wrote his thought down.

Nina watched him the whole time. He looked up at her and winked and then added three more words to his note. "Do you have any envelopes?"

"Yes." She opened the drawer she'd been rummaging in when he first saw her the other night and handed him an envelope. "Do you need a stamp?"

"No," he began. Then he changed his mind. "In fact, yes. Let's mail it. You can't open it when it arrives, but that way you'll know that what you see inside there is what I just wrote today."

She gave him a puzzled look. "Is this some FBI thing?"

He laughed. "No, it's just a Manny thing, but I hope that someday you'll think it's a good thing."

"Are you going to explain?"

He shook his head. It was probably a terrible idea, but he couldn't get rid of the feeling that it was one of the best ideas he'd ever had. "Trust me? Just wait and see?"

"I trust you."

He already knew it, but her words strengthened his conviction.

~ ~ ~

Nina glanced over at Manny as he drove. She wanted to pinch herself to make sure that this was real—that she wasn't dreaming the whole thing. Could she really be riding in the car with this gorgeous man who was making no secret of the fact that he was attracted to her? Did they really have a month laid out ahead of them when they'd share her house and have all the time and space they needed to get to know each other?

Given the fact that just a few days ago she'd still been living and working in Stanton Falls—and trying to avoid a creepy guy who was too attracted to her—it all felt a little too good to be true.

Manny smiled when he felt her looking at him. "Are you okay?"

"I'm great. Just admiring the view." She smiled as she said it, knowing that he'd probably assume that she meant the view of the lake as they passed.

"It is a beautiful little town," he agreed and glanced out of his window at the blue water that sparkled under the afternoon sun before fixing his gaze back on the road. "It's good that you can still appreciate that."

"I try not to take anything for granted. I've lived here all my life and so have most of my friends. A lot of them don't notice anymore. They're so busy going about their lives, they get caught up in the details and the everyday problems. I try to remember that no matter what's going wrong, at least it's happening with a beautiful backdrop of the mountains and the lake. At least, I'm not stuck in an apartment in some dark, gray city somewhere."

Manny smiled at that. "That's a good outlook to have."

"It is. It's not always easy, but it helps. There's always something to be grateful for if you remember to look for it. It's easier for me at the moment, too. Stanton Falls is a pretty little town. But it's not like the lake. Having been gone helps me appreciate being back. It's like seeing the place with new eyes."

She glanced over at him again. "It's all new to your eyes, isn't it? How do you see it?"

He pursed his lips before he spoke. "It's not brand new. I was here for a month a while back."

Nina frowned. Had she known that? "What were you here for?"

"Work. I helped Diego's son, Zack, out."

"Oh!" She had known about that. Abbie had told her Zack's story of how the man who'd been tracking him down to kill him had been caught and arrested. It was strange to make the connection that Manny was the guy who'd done the arresting.

He smiled. "It's different now. Now, I get to see the place from a different perspective. Back then I looked at the town, the lake, the trails, everything, as the setting for an investigation. The details I noticed were all about what might happen. Now, I can see them for what they are and appreciate the beauty."

The way he glanced over at her as he spoke the last few words made her feel as though he was including her as part of the beauty he could see. She smiled. Whether or not that was his intention, he made her feel beautiful—and that was something that hadn't happened in far too long.

He turned off East Shore Road when they reached the lodge at Four Mile Creek and pulled into the parking lot at the shopping plaza.

When he cut the engine, she raised an eyebrow at him, making him laugh. "I know we were going to head back to the house … and we can if you'd like. But I thought you might want to have a look around here first?"

She nodded happily. "I'd love to. I like it over here, but this place is still new to me. It's only been here a couple of years and …" She frowned. Not wanting to explain that Paul had died just before the lodge opened and she hadn't gone anywhere much in the months after that. Then she'd moved up to Stanton.

He held her gaze for a moment and she felt as though he knew what she was thinking, but he didn't comment on it. Instead, he smiled. "Good. I like the idea that we can get to know this place together, not just have you show me around your town."

She smiled back. She liked that idea, too.

They walked down the cobbled pathway that wound between the stores and led to the central plaza.

Manny raised an eyebrow at her. "Would you rather sit and have a drink or browse the stores?"

She had to laugh. "My guess is that you're not much of a browser. Shall we go to the café?"

The corners of his lips twitched up. "You got me. I'm not much of a shopper, but my guess is that you are … and I like seeing you enjoy yourself."

His words made her heart clench in her chest and she stopped walking to look up at him.

His frown was back. "Did I say something wrong?"

She shook her head and had to blink her eyes a couple times before she spoke. "No. You couldn't have said anything more right. You just took me by surprise. I'm not used to …" She didn't want to spell out the fact that Paul hadn't shown much interest in what she enjoyed and he certainly hadn't been prepared to put aside his own wants to see her enjoy herself. She knew now that he had, in fact, done the exact opposite. He'd set aside any care for what she wanted while he ensured that he'd enjoyed himself—with Lorraine.

Manny was watching her face intently. "I take it you're not going to finish that sentence?"

She shook her head slowly.

He nodded and placed his hand in the small of her back guiding her as he started walking again. "That's okay. I'm not used to having the company of a beautiful woman or the pleasure of seeing her enjoy herself. So, indulge me? Where do you want to start?"

She looked into his eyes for a long moment, wanting to tell him that she was already enjoying every moment she was spending with him; the rest didn't really matter.

"Manny!" A shadow crossed his face when the sound of his name being called broke the moment. He recovered quickly and gave her a rueful smile as he turned.

"Zack! How are you?"

Zack grinned at them. "Great thanks. What are you guys up to?"

Nina smiled at him. She didn't know him all that well. He was one of Abbie's group of friends. A pilot, Diego's son, and from what she knew of him, a fine young man.

"Nina's being kind enough to show me around. We took a hike up above Four Mile and now we're here to explore the plaza and have a drink."

Zack smiled at her. "That's awesome." He held out his hand. "I know you're Abbie's mom, but I don't think we've ever actually been introduced. "I'm Zack."

She smiled back as she shook with him. "I know. It's good to see you. How's Maria?"

"She's great, thanks. She'd been working this morning. I've come to get her."

"Well, give her my best, won't you?" said Manny. "We won't keep you."

Nina could tell by the look on Zack's face that he'd been hoping to keep them to talk a while. The half-smile he gave Manny said that he understood.

"Will do. It's good to see you." He nodded at Nina. "It's good to see you, too. I heard you were back."

"It's good to be back."

"Well, I'll give you a call, Manny. Maria's been talking about getting you over for dinner. It's weird for you to be in town and not be staying at our place."

Manny laughed. "It is weird, but I like it better this way."

Zack nodded enthusiastically. "Me too!" He laughed when saw the expression on Nina's face. "Don't get me wrong. I love him and everything … I can vouch that he's a wonderful house guest. What I like better is that now he's here because he wants to be … not because my life's depending on him."

Nina smiled and nodded as if she understood, but she wasn't sure that she did. It was one thing to know that she trusted Manny, that he made her feel safe. It was another to realize that it was more than just a feeling. It was completely justified. He'd saved Zack's life in a very real way. And now she thought about it, he'd no doubt saved many others, too.

Manny turned to her once Zack had gone. "Sorry about that."

"Why?"

He shrugged. "Honestly, I thought we'd be less likely to run into people over here."

"It's okay. I don't mind. I'm not trying to avoid people. I know I said this morning that I didn't want to go to breakfast because I wasn't looking forward to explaining why I'm back here, but ..." She stopped when she saw the way he was looking at her. "What?"

He smiled through pursed lips. "I understand that. My point was that I want you all to myself."

"Oh." As she looked up into his eyes, the already familiar feel of butterflies stirred in her stomach. She wanted him all to herself, too.

Chapter Nine

Manny pulled the front door closed behind him quietly, then waited for a moment hoping that he hadn't disturbed Nina. It was too early. He glanced at his watch and wasn't surprised to see that it was a quarter till six—his usual time to run before work on the days when he was in the office and not out in the field somewhere. He might officially be retired now, but his body apparently, hadn't gotten the memo.

He walked up the path and closed the gate behind him, turning to glance up at the bedroom window. He didn't want to wake her because he knew that she'd have to get up soon anyway. She had to get up and go to work. He shook his head and started to jog down the street.

She'd gotten a call yesterday afternoon while they drove back from the plaza. Apparently, she was a stand-in for the cleaning crew at the resort here in town. He couldn't help frowning as he jogged on. He hated that she needed to do that. She hadn't spelled out her financial situation. They hadn't even talked about it, but it didn't take much figuring out. She'd lost her job in Stanton Falls and had come back home. When he'd offered to move out, she'd admitted that she didn't want to lose the rent. And when she'd gotten that call to go in and clean rooms at the resort today, she'd sounded eager when she'd said that yes, she could be there at seven.

Manny didn't understand—and he knew he probably shouldn't even be wondering—why she needed the work so badly. He would have thought that after a marriage that had lasted half a lifetime, she should be provided for well enough that she didn't need to work.

He picked up his pace as he crossed the square at the resort. He shouldn't even be thinking about it. This was the first Monday morning of his retirement. He should be focused on the present moment, enjoying the fact that he could enjoy his run without keeping an eye on the time. He should be thinking about his future that now lay before him, allowing him to do whatever he chose. He pursed his lips. The trouble was, thinking about Nina felt like he was thinking about his future.

He knew it would sound crazy if he told anyone else what he was thinking. No one—least of all him—was expecting him to find himself a woman once he retired. It just didn't fit with who he was. His vision of his retirement had included finding some purpose, maybe some part-time freelance work. But it hadn't included meeting someone, especially not allowing himself to care about someone.

He slowed his pace when he saw a man come out of one of the gates a little farther up Main Street. He tried to figure out if he should know who it was. If he should, he didn't. The man turned in his direction and frowned when he saw him. He jogged on the spot for a few moments and then stretched his quads while Manny approached.

"Morning."

"Morning." Manny nodded but didn't stop. He wasn't sure he wanted company on his run this morning, and this guy was giving off a weird vibe.

He wasn't surprised when he fell in beside him.

"You're Manny, right?"

"That's me." He glanced at the guy. "You?"

"I'm Ivan."

Ah. That explained the weird vibe. Manny smiled. All of a sudden it was important to win him over. He was Abbie's fiancé. From everything she'd said, Nina saw him as a son-in-law already, and a much loved one at that. She'd already warned him that Ivan didn't approve of their house-sharing situation.

"It's good to meet you."

Ivan nodded, and Manny liked him for not immediately claiming the same thing. It seemed that Ivan would rather reserve judgment about whether it was a pleasure until he got to know him.

They ran on in silence until they reached the park at the end of Main Street. Manny had run this route a few times when he'd been here before. He knew that they would come out on the old road by the river—where they'd finally brought Morales down.

"Do you want some company?" asked Ivan.

"Sure." Manny smiled. "I think we can probably sidestep all the bullshit, can't we?"

Ivan gave him a puzzled look.

"I mean we should probably just admit that you need to scope me out and see if you want me around your mother-in-law, and I need to get to know you and to show you that I can be trusted."

Ivan smiled. "Yeah, in that case, I think we *can* sidestep the bullshit. I've heard nothing but good things about you. But I'm sure you can understand, I need to know for myself."

"I don't just understand, I'm glad of it. I'm glad she has you to watch her back."

"I want to, but …" They ran on in silence for a while before Ivan looked at him again. "Don't screw with her, okay?"

"I give you my word."

They emerged on the other side of the park and started up the hill. It was steep enough that further conversation wasn't an option until the road leveled off again.

"What is this for you?"

"What do you mean?" Manny asked.

"I mean, are just here for a month and looking to … enjoy Nina's company before you leave? Or are you thinking you're really going to move here?"

"Which would you rather it was?"

Ivan shrugged. "Honestly? I don't know."

Manny felt for him. He was trying to look out for Nina, but it seemed that he didn't have much of a clue how to go about it.

"Let me see if I can put your mind at ease, then. You're worried about her, and I can appreciate that. But I don't want you to worry. In fact, I'd like to think that I might gain your approval, maybe even support … yours and Abbie's. So, I'll lay it all on the line for you."

"If you'd asked me on Friday afternoon, I'd have told you that I was just here for the month. That I liked the idea of making this place my home, but if I had to put money on it, then I'd say it wouldn't work out that way. I would also have told you that meeting a woman wasn't something that was on my radar."

Ivan glanced at him and slowed to a walk. He pointed to a bench up ahead on the side of the road. "Do you want to sit for a while?"

"Sure."

When they reached the bench, Ivan sat, but Manny stayed on his feet and began to pace in front of him. Ivan couldn't know it, but the guys back at the office would have warned him that a pacing Manny was an agitated Manny.

"So, what changed?" asked Ivan.

Manny had to smile. "Everything. I don't know if you'll be able to understand this, but ... I told you I wasn't looking for a woman, but from the first moment ..." He didn't want to tell Ivan that the first moment he'd met Nina, he'd grabbed her from behind in her own kitchen, thinking that she was a burglar. He shook his head to clear it, feeling sure that Ivan would somehow pick up on what he was thinking—about the way she'd felt in his arms when he'd held her against him to stop her from escaping.

"There's just something about her. She's fragile, but strong. She's kind and easy-going." He smiled as he remembered their morning coffee. "I tend to think of women as needing more attention and more conversation than I have to offer. Nina's not like that. She ... she doesn't need a damned thing from me, but she makes me want to give her everything. She thinks she can stand on her own two feet, but that just makes me want to ensure she doesn't have to."

He felt pretty damned foolish when Ivan looked up at him through narrowed eyes. He wanted to elaborate, to explain that he knew how crazy that must sound after only having known her for a few days. Instead, he waited. Ivan's expression didn't bode well.

"Have you looked into her past?"

Manny hadn't expected that. He didn't know if he was more surprised at Ivan for asking or at himself that the thought hadn't even occurred to him.

"No."

Ivan raised an eyebrow.

"I haven't. And that tells me—even if it doesn't tell you—just how off-kilter she has me. Why? What do I need to know?"

"Nah." Ivan waved a hand at him. "It's not mine to tell. It's not even mine to know. I wish that I didn't know myself."

"Know what?"

Ivan blew out a sigh. "About Paul."

"What about him? I thought Abbie didn't know."

"Know what?"

Manny finally sat down on the bench beside Ivan. He clasped his hands together and stared out at the lake. "I have the feeling that we're going to be friends, you and I, more than friends someday maybe. So, no bullshit. Nina hasn't said but has given away enough that I know that Paul wasn't a saint, and that their marriage wasn't … the best. But she also told me that she'd kept that hidden from Abbie because she adored her father. Now, you're telling me that you wished you didn't know what you know about him, so. Ah …" Now he thought he understood. Ivan knew something about Paul, but Abbie didn't.

Ivan nodded. "I shouldn't have gone digging. But there were little things that didn't add up. Abbie was away in the city for the last several years Paul was alive. She still thinks of him the way she wants to remember him: as a good guy, loving husband, and father. I'm not sure he ever was that."

"So, what was he?" Manny's heart was pounding. Nina had told him that her marriage hadn't been happy. He'd hoped that one day she'd tell him more. He knew he shouldn't be learning the details from anyone other than her. But he needed to know what Ivan had to say.

"He had a long-term affair. Like, twelve years. He had his girlfriend set up in an apartment down in Abbottsville. He'd syphoned off all of their savings. Left Nina with next to nothing—other than a bunch of debts. Nina never told Abbie about it. Abbie came back and helped her get back on feet—financially and emotionally—after he died. I didn't meet Abbie until after that. At first, I believed the way she told it—she still does—but it just didn't add up. Nina should have been comfortable after he died, not up to her eyeballs in debt. So, I did some digging. I found out about the girlfriend. Turns out he died at her place. Massive heart attack after he got off the phone with Nina."

Manny blew out a sigh. "How?"

"How did I find out? I'd rather not say. I lied some and I'm not proud of that, but I talked to the girlfriend and she told me everything."

"Nina doesn't know that you know?"

Ivan shook his head. "Like I said. I wish I didn't know. The two of them are my family now. I never really had one before. And it sucks that I know more about her father than Abbie does, and I know all about what Nina still thinks is a secret."

Manny nodded. "Not an enviable situation you find yourself in."

"Yeah, but I put myself here. I wanted to understand, but now I wish I didn't." He turned to look at Manny. "And I feel like a shit because now you know, and you shouldn't. If you and Nina are going to get together, then she should tell you herself if she wants you to know. And if you're not, then you have no right to know."

"Yeah." Nina had told him that her marriage hadn't been happy. She'd even told him that she hadn't admitted that to anyone else. He hoped that maybe she'd get around to telling him the whole story at some point. But Ivan was right. It was hers to tell. He shouldn't know it.

He felt bad for the kid.

"What did you mean when you said that you and I might become friends … more than friends?"

Manny stared out at the lake. "At risk of making you think I'm crazy, I already know that I want to be with her. I can't tell her that yet. I'd scare the crap out of her, I know. But since you shared with me. I'm sharing with you. I didn't know what my retirement was going to be about. Now I do. It's going to be about Nina."

Ivan smiled at him. "It does sound crazy, but for some reason, I believe you."

"If it's any consolation. I've proved out every hunch I ever had in the last eighteen years. Working at the bureau. When I finally learned to trust my gut, I got good at it. We'd go into a situation and I'd get an idea of how it was going to pan out. I was right every time. It didn't always happen. But whenever I did get a hunch, a feeling, a knowing, if you like, it always panned out."

"I thought that when I retired, I'd lose that. But it's the feeling I've had about Nina. We're going to be together; we're meant to be together. I'm in no hurry. But I have no doubt."

"On the one hand, that sounds awesome," said Ivan. "Part of me hopes that this hunch of yours pans out. On the other hand …"

The silence lengthened so long that Manny had to break it. "On the other hand, what?"

Ivan let out a short laugh. "It sounds creepy as fuck!"

Manny had to laugh. "I guess it does, huh?" He shrugged. "That's why I didn't plan to say anything at all. I can just wait and see. If I'm wrong, if she doesn't see me that way, I can accept that. I'll bow out. I'm not going to be like—" Shit! He'd been about to say that he wasn't another Brian. But then he remembered that she hadn't told Abbie and Ivan about Brian because she didn't want to worry them.

Ivan was frowning at him. "You're not going to be like what?"

Manny shook his head.

"C'mon. You can't do that to me."

Manny blew out a sigh. "Are we just screwing this up right from the get-go? You told me one of Nina's secrets. I'm about to tell you another."

"So, tell me."

"Part of the reason that she's back here is that she had a creepy dude up in Stanton Falls."

"Who? What do you mean? Abbie hasn't said anything."

"Abbie doesn't know. Nina went on a date with a guy. She didn't much like him, but her friend persuaded her to go out with him a second time. After that, she told him that she didn't want to see him again, but he didn't want to take no for an answer. He grabbed her in the alley outside the store the other night. That's mostly why she came home."

"Damn. And she didn't want to upset Abbie, so she didn't say anything?"

"Yep. So, you can see why the last thing I want to be is another creepy guy going after her when she's not interested?"

Ivan let out a short laugh. "Yeah."

They sat in silence for a long while, staring out at the lake, each lost in their own thoughts.

"So, where does this leave us?" Manny asked eventually.

"I'd say it makes us a team. We're bound together by secrets and I believe we both have her best interests at heart. I even feel better about your living arrangements now."

"You do?"

"Yeah. I hate to think of that guy from Stanton coming down here after her. Did they lock him up?"

Manny frowned. It wasn't like him, but he hadn't followed up on what she'd told him about Brian. To be fair, given that it was Monday morning, this was the first chance he'd had. "I'm going to talk to the sheriff this morning."

Ivan checked his watch. "I'd better be getting back. I need to get to work. Will you let me know what he says?"

"Sure. Do you want to give me your number?"

After they'd exchanged numbers, they ran back the way they'd come. It was too late now to complete the entire loop. Ivan needed to get to work and Manny wanted to take a shower and then head into the sheriff's office to talk to Don.

Chapter Ten

Teresa opened the door with a big grin, and Nina couldn't help but smile back at her.

"Come on in, girlfriend. I have wine, I have munchies, and I want to hear all about it. I can't believe that you've managed to avoid me since the weekend. I'm bursting to hear all your news."

Nina laughed as she followed her friend through to the kitchen where Teresa handed her a glass of wine.

"Do you want to sit outside? It's cooled off a little."

"Okay."

Once they were seated at the table out on the patio, Teresa leaned forward on her elbows. "Come on, then. Tell me everything."

Nina laughed. "Well, for starters, I haven't been avoiding you. You should know better than that."

Teresa waved a hand. "Of course, I do. But I also know that saying it will encourage you to open up and tell me everything."

"You're terrible."

"I never denied it. So, tell me?"

Nina let out a big happy sigh. "He's lovely, Terry."

"Aww. Look at you!"

Nina felt her cheeks color. "Sorry, that sounds really sappy I know, but he is. He might look all big and mean and muscly, but he's so gentle and kind."

Teresa rolled her eyes. "Don't. That's just not fair. I want to hear what the two of you have been up to. I want to live vicariously through your sex-life, not pine for the kind of man I'll never have."

"Don't say that. You'll meet someone someday."

"Ha! Right. Whatever. Tell me about the good stuff. What's he like?"

Nina laughed. "I told you. He's lovely."

"I mean in bed!"

"I know you do. But I can't tell you."

"Seriously? You're both obviously infatuated with each other. You're living under the same roof and have been for nearly a week now. Why haven't you slept with him?"

Nina rolled her eyes. "Not because I don't want to, believe me."

Teresa frowned. "Don't tell me he doesn't want to. I'm not buying that. You could tell just from the way he was looking at you last weekend at the Boathouse. He would have done you that night if you'd given him the green light."

Nina took a sip of her wine. "I know."

"Oh, good. You're not denying it then?"

"No. I'm … honestly? I don't know what I'm doing. Other than, I'm taking my time, and so's he. This week has been weird. I've ended up working twelve hour shifts at the resort. So, I haven't had the time or energy for anything else. He's finding his feet here, that was always his plan. And besides, there's no rush."

"No rush? He's only here for a month. If I were you, I'd be making the most of it, not wasting half the time building up to it."

"But you're not me, and I'm not you. It's all good, as far as I'm concerned. In the little bits of time that we see each other, it's … nice. We're getting to know each other."

"Has anything at all happened between the two of you? Does he even know that you're interested?"

Nina dropped her gaze.

"Oh, my God! What does that mean?"

She laughed. "It means that we've kissed … quite a lot. He told me that he wants to see what can happen between us. And I told him I'd like that, too."

"So, make something happen already!"

She met her friend's gaze. "I think I'm going to."

"What? When?"

"Well, I'm finishing work at four tomorrow and then I'm off for at least the weekend. I've been working such a lot because they needed cover in the gift shop. But the usual weekend staff will be in from tomorrow afternoon. I don't know when they'll need me again. So, I was thinking that I could make him dinner tomorrow night."

Teresa nodded eagerly. "Better yet, get him to take you out to dinner. A few glasses of wine and then ..."

Nina chuckled. "You have to remember that this is a big deal for me."

"I know it is. Come on, Nina. We've been friends since kindergarten. I know full well that you've never slept with anyone but Paul. That's why I'm so eager for you and Manny to get together. He's such a good guy. You should make the most of him while he's here. There are loads of losers out there who'd sleep with you at the drop of a hat. At our age, there aren't many good guys left who aren't already taken."

"I know. It just seems so fast. I've only known him for a week."

"So what? You'll only know him for another three weeks at this rate, and you don't want to be kicking yourself after he leaves for all the time that you've wasted."

Nina sipped her wine. She hated the thought—even though she knew that it was a distinct possibility—that when September rolled around, Manny would leave and that would be it. Teresa was right, though. If he did, she'd rather be left with memories of what they'd shared than with regrets that she hadn't been brave enough to share his bed.

Teresa patted her arm. "What's he doing tonight?"

"He's at his friend's house. Ted and Audrey invited a bunch of people over."

Teresa opened her mouth, but Nina held up her hand, knowing what she was about to say.

"Yes. He did invite me to go with him. But you know me better than that. I'm nervous enough about going out with him. I don't feel confident to get to know him in front of all his friends. I'm not saying I won't ever. I really like Izzy and Audrey, and I already know Chris quite well from the center. But I haven't exactly had a social life for a long time. I need to take one step at a time."

"Okay. I get it. I won't give you any grief if you start taking the steps. Tomorrow night, you take Manny to bed. After that, you can start hanging out with his friends."

She had to laugh. "I'll go in my own good time, thank you. Anyway, I don't want to spend the whole evening talking about that. What's going on with you?"

"Nothing much. The salon's still busy. The girls still keep the grapevine buzzing with everything they overhear." Teresa smiled. "I'm happy to tell you that the Summer Lake gossip mongers have you and Manny a lot further ahead in your relationship than you are."

Nina rolled her eyes. "Of course, they do. What are they saying?"

"That the two of you got together the night he arrived and that you're getting married."

Nina almost choked on her wine. "What?!"

Teresa grinned. "I know, right? As if you'd sleep with him on the first night?"

Nina gave her a stern look.

"Don't look at me like that. If you get your act together, I can see the two of you getting married and you getting to have the happily ever after you always deserved. But only if you get your act together and dive in. If you tiptoe around, the month will fly by, and he'll be gone before you understand what you've lost."

"I'm not even going to … I can't even … married?!" Nina blew out a short laugh. "Now, that is crazy. But I have decided that I'm going to make the most of the time he's here. And I'm hoping that he won't leave at the end of the month. He was already considering staying."

"Then make sure that he wants to."

Nina nodded. She was hoping that she could.

It was only a little after nine when she got home. It was early, but she needed to be at the gift shop by six in the morning. It was crazy busy in there. She'd been happy to help out when Ben had asked her on Monday. The manager had gone home sick at lunchtime and Ben had come to find Nina when she was finishing up in the laundry. She'd worked in the gift shop a few summers before Paul died. So, it worked out well, she knew how to manage the place, and she enjoyed it.

She went through to the kitchen and turned the light on, smiling to herself when she saw a note propped up on the counter. She hadn't seen much of Manny since Sunday. She left before he was up in the mornings and in the evenings, she'd barely been able to keep her eyes open long enough to eat. He'd asked if she wanted to go with him to Ted and Audrey's this evening, but she'd already promised Teresa that she'd visit with her for a while. She wouldn't have gone with him anyway.

But for all she hadn't seen him, she was still very aware that he was around. He'd left her little notes every day. They'd only been a few words, just letting her know what he was up to, or that he hoped her day went well. Each morning, she'd come down to find the coffee pot all set up and ready to brew. This morning, he'd even left her a cinnamon scone. That had to have been a lucky guess. He couldn't know that they were her favorites.

Her smile grew bigger as she read this note.

Sleep well. Hope to see you tomorrow—night?

Manny.

She hoped so, too. Teresa said that she should ask him out to dinner. But she'd much rather stay in and cook for him.

She reached for the pad and wrote a reply.

I hope so, too. I'll cook dinner – if you like?

Nina

She set the note where his had been and then wondered if he would realize that it wasn't the one he'd left. She moved it farther along the countertop and then went upstairs. It might be early, but she needed sleep.

She'd just gotten into bed when she heard the front door open. It made her smile. It was good to know he was home. Well, this wasn't his home. But it was good to know he was here. She couldn't help but remember the nights when her heart would sink when she heard the door and knew that Paul was home. She hadn't known then where he spent all his nights when he was away. She'd naively believed him that his job required a lot more travel than it really did.

She gave herself a shake. She didn't need to dwell on the past and all the sadness. She was right here in the present, and so was Manny. She didn't dare think about the future.

She heard a creak on the stairs. That wasn't like him. The house was old. It had its quirks, but Manny had figured out very quickly how to move around silently. Maybe he'd had a few drinks and wasn't thinking?

She smiled when she heard a soft tap on the door.

"Are you awake?"

"Yes. Come on in." She bit down on her lip as soon as she'd said it. So far, they'd each respected the other's space. She hadn't gone near his room—even though it had been her room for decades. He hadn't come near hers. It had seemed more appropriate to keep everything downstairs.

The door swung open slowly and her breath caught in her chest at the sight of him. He smiled and leaned against the doorframe, folding his arms across his chest.

"Hi." It came out as more of a squeak than a word, but it was all she could manage. It seemed that her body was so busy reacting to the sight of him that it didn't have enough focus left to make her voice work properly.

The way he smiled at her sent shivers chasing each other down her back. She held the sheet closer to her chest, glad that he couldn't see what she could feel—the way her nipples stood to attention.

"Hi. I didn't mean to disturb you."

"It's okay. You didn't." That wasn't entirely true. He disturbed her peace of mind, he made her want to squirm in her panties. But he hadn't disturbed her in the sense that he meant. She pulled herself together. "I just got into bed. Did you have a good evening?"

"I did." He held her gaze for a long moment. "It would have been better if you were there."

It felt so good to hear him say it. She smiled. "Tomorrow night. I left you a note …"

"I saw it." He frowned, and her heart sank.

"It's okay if you have other plans. I didn't mean … I don't …" She dropped her gaze. She felt stupid now.

She bit down on the inside of her lip when she sensed him come into the room. He stopped at the edge of the bed and waited until she looked up at him. His eyes burned with an intensity she hadn't seen in them before.

"May I sit?"

She nodded, unable to tear her eyes away from his as he sat on the edge of the bed. He reached for her hand but didn't take it. She understood; that was the way he'd been with everything between them. He made clear what he wanted but waited for her to let him know it was what she wanted, too. She tentatively took his hand, and then relaxed a little when his strong warm fingers closed around hers.

As he sat there holding her small hand in his, Manny had to remind himself that he was a man who exercised self-control in all things. Right now, all he wanted to do was get into bed with her, hold her, let her know that she was safe with him, that she'd always be safe with him. Then when she relaxed enough in his arms that he knew she believed him, he wanted to explore her body, to make a start on a journey of getting to know each other better that he hoped would last the rest of their lives.

But no. Self-control. He met her gaze. "Sorry. I'm blowing it again. I don't have other plans. I was hoping that we could make plans. I'm assuming that you backtracked because I frowned?"

She nodded.

"Yeah. Apparently, that's a bad habit of mine. It doesn't mean that I'm angry about anything, though. Usually, what it means is that I'm pissed at myself. Or that I want to make a suggestion but I'm not sure of the best way to do it."

"What did that frown just mean then?"

"It didn't mean that I don't want to have dinner with you. There's nothing I want more." Well, that wasn't entirely true. But he shouldn't think about or mention what he really wanted while he was sitting here on her bed. "It meant that I don't want you to have to cook. I thought I could take you out. We could go to a place called Giuseppe's if you like it. I heard it's much quieter than the Boathouse."

To his relief, she relaxed. "I really don't mind cooking. I enjoy it. It helps me relax. Honestly, after the week I've had at work, I wouldn't look forward to going out." She squeezed his hand. "But I will look forward to staying in, with you."

His eyes darted up to meet hers. With another woman he would have understood what she meant—what she was hinting at. To his surprise, Nina was blushing deep red. Apparently, it was what she meant too. He shifted in his pants as his cock sprang to life. Despite her obvious embarrassment, she didn't look away. She held his gaze and nodded slowly. Damn, she was beautiful.

He couldn't help it. He leaned toward her and gently brushed his lips over hers. "I told you, Nina. I don't want to rush you."

She took him by surprise, sending shock waves rushing through him when she nipped his bottom lip and breathed. "Maybe I want to rush you."

He put his hands on her shoulders and leaned back so that he could see her face. He was gratified to see that although her cheeks were still flushed, there was no mistaking the desire in her eyes.

He smiled. "You do, huh?"

"I do. I should warn you that I don't even know how to play games. I only know how to keep my mouth shut or speak my mind. So far, I've kept my mouth shut because I thought I must be out of my mind. But now I know, Manny. I want … I want …"

His cock throbbed against his zipper as he waited to hear what word she'd choose.

"I want you," she finished.

He pulled her toward him, closing his arms around her and claiming her mouth in a kiss that should leave her with no doubt that the feeling was mutual. When he finally lifted his head, he smiled down at her. "In case you didn't understand what I just said—"

She surprised him again when she cut him off. "I did. Message received, loud and clear. You want me, too."

He chuckled, thrilled that she wasn't nearly so shy or unsure of herself as he'd led himself to believe.

He cupped his hand around the back of her neck and brushed his thumb over her nape, loving the way she closed her eyes and let out a small sigh.

"I want you so much … But …" Her eyes flew open on the but, just as he'd expected they would. He continued to stroke her nape with his thumb. Hoping that would reassure her. This wasn't rejection—far from it. "But I've waited this long, I'd like to wait until tomorrow."

He knew he should feel bad but the disappointment in her eyes made him happy.

"If you say now, I won't argue. But you have to be up early for work in the morning. So, I'll have to let you get some sleep. If we wait until tomorrow, I can romance you all evening and then love you all night."

The way she shifted made him guess that she was pressing her thighs together and the thought that his words could turn her on had him wanting to take back everything he'd just said and get under the covers with her.

She met his gaze and nodded. "Now I'm really going to look forward to tomorrow night."

He brushed his thumb over her lips, not daring to risk kissing her again. "Me, too".

Chapter Eleven

Nina was relieved to find the house empty when she got home from work. It wasn't that she didn't want to see Manny. She was excited about the evening ahead, but she wanted to shower and get changed. She was dirty and sweaty after a busy day in the gift store that had seen her crawling around in the storage room in the back twice looking for inventory that was logged as being there, but she'd be damned if she could find.

Before she'd left this afternoon, Ben had stopped in to ask if she'd mind covering again next week. She was grateful for the work—and even more grateful that he'd arranged someone to cover the evenings. She'd still have to go in at seven and open up, but she'd be able to leave at five. That still meant ten-hour days, but she needed the money, and she'd have her evenings free. Of course, she was hoping that she'd spend at least some of them with Manny.

She set her purse down on the counter in the kitchen and sat down for a minute. She should have stopped at the grocery store on the way home. She'd need to go back out again, but she had to take a shower first.

She dug for her phone when it rang, her heart racing. Her first thought was that it might be Manny saying that he couldn't make it tonight after all, but no, that was just nerves. He was looking forward to this evening and she knew it. She frowned until her fingers closed around her phone. Perhaps it was Abbie wanting to come over. How could she turn her down if it were? She shook her head at herself. So much for trying to see the bright side. Why was she looking for the worst when it came to her evening ahead with Manny?

When she finally got a look at the display, she was relieved but surprised to see it was Janet calling. She hadn't been in touch since the day Nina left Stanton.

"Hi, Janet," she answered. "What's up?"

"Hi, Nina. How are you?"

"I'm doing well, thanks. How about you?"

"Yeah. I'm fine. Listen, this … I don't know how to tell you this."

Nina frowned. "What? Just go ahead and say it whatever it is."

Janet sighed. "I'm sorry. I …"

"Oh, just tell me already." Nina surprised herself with the sharp edge to her voice, but she was a little irritated with Janet over the way things had gone. She didn't have time for beating around the bush. She wanted to get off the phone and get ready for her evening.

"Okay. There's no need to be like that. You need to know that Brian was in the store today."

"Oh." Nina sat back down heavily. She'd done well to put him completely out of her mind since she came home. She hadn't wanted to think about what he'd done in the alley—or what he might have done if she hadn't managed to get away—

if those guys hadn't been right there. Perhaps it wasn't healthy that she'd decided to put the whole incident out of her mind. Just hearing his name made her hands tremble.

"Yeah. I'm surprised he had the nerve to show his face."

"What … what did he want? Did he say anything?"

"He did, but not to me. He was asking Kerry about you."

"Asking what? She didn't tell him anything, did she?"

"Well …"

"Janet!"

"I'm sorry, Nina. She didn't know."

"She didn't know? You didn't tell her what happened?"

"I didn't want to spook her. I didn't want … I'm sorry. I didn't want word to get out that there was … someone like that hanging around my store. And I mean, he's not a danger. It's not as though he was going to attack women in general. It was you he was interested in."

Nina clutched her phone tightly in her hand. It was obvious that Janet's number one priority had been to make sure that no one was scared away from her store. That was apparently more important to her than keeping people safe.

She closed her eyes as a thought struck her. "So, Kerry didn't know that she shouldn't talk to him? What did she tell him?"

"I'm sorry, Nina. He made out like he was just a customer, asked after you and where you'd been this week. Kerry didn't know any better. She told him that you'd gone home."

Nina dropped her head. "And she told him where home is." It wasn't a question.

"Not your address or anything!"

"As if that makes much of a difference."

"It'd be a whole lot worse if she had."

Nina didn't think so. If he was crazy enough to come here after her, it wouldn't take him long to find out where she lived. Summer Lake was a small town. People here were friendly. They wouldn't think there was any reason to be wary of someone looking for her.

She bit her tongue; there was no point in giving Janet the mouthful she deserved. "Well, thank you for letting me know."

"I'm sorry, Nina. Really, I am. I thought he would know where you're from anyway. You went out with him twice. Hopefully, him asking doesn't mean anything. He's curious but he wouldn't do anything."

"What, just like he was curious when he was visiting your store looking for me? We both know what he did after that."

"I'm sorry."

"So am I." She had to stop herself from reassuring Janet that it was okay. Her instincts were always to reassure people, to make them feel better—to tell them it wasn't their fault. But in this case, she wouldn't allow herself to do it. She didn't know that it would be okay, and she didn't want to make Janet feel better because this really was her fault.

"What are you going to do? Should you maybe go to the police there? I'd feel better if they knew to be on the lookout for him."

Nina thought about it; it might not be a bad idea to have a chat with the sheriff. She'd known Don all her life. She felt a little of the tension ease in her shoulders when she realized that she had someone much closer to home who would make her feel better if he were keeping an eye on her.

"I'll figure something out. I have to go."

"All right. Are we okay?"

Nina pursed her lips. She didn't have it in her to hold a grudge, but she knew that their friendship wouldn't be the same after this. It had already shifted with what had happened last week, but the fact that Janet had been more concerned about her store than about Nina's safety … "We're fine."

"You're not going to come back in October, are you?"

"No. You're going to need to find someone else. I have to go, Janet."

"Okay. I'm really sorry. I'll call you. Bye."

Nina knew that she probably wouldn't. She set her phone down on the counter with a sigh. Brian wouldn't show up here at the lake, would he? God, she hoped not. She'd tell Manny about it. She had to. He was living at her house too. He needed to know that there might be someone coming around. That wasn't all though. She'd told him that first night at the Boathouse that she couldn't think of anyone she'd rather have come to her rescue. It was true. The thought of Brian coming scared her, but knowing that Manny was here made her feel safe anyway.

~ ~ ~

"Are you sure you're not going to bring the lovely Nina out with everyone tonight?" asked Diego.

Manny smiled at him. "I am absolutely sure. But you guys have a good time."

Diego smirked at him. "We will. We always do. But you can't keep hiding her away. The girls want to get to know her. I want to get her on my side to make sure that she's going to be one more reason to make you stay here."

Manny laughed and looked back over his shoulder at the others who were all sitting out on the back deck of Diego and

Izzy's house. He'd had a good time with them this afternoon and he'd stayed as long as he could stand it. It was probably too early now even but he couldn't make himself wait any longer before he went back to Nina's place.

Diego was walking him out to his car. "She's the biggest reason."

Diego grinned and grasped his shoulder. "I know. I can see it. So, why not let us help you?"

"I don't need any help. What I need is some time with her. Time alone. She's not someone who wants or needs to be part of a group all the time."

"Like you, then?"

He nodded. "I suppose. I'm enjoying my time hanging out with you guys. But she doesn't know you and she's still finding her feet—after her husband died and after coming back here again."

"Okay. I'll be good. I won't keep harassing you. Just know that I … we … want you to stay, and we'd love it if you and Nina get together." Diego chuckled. "It's funny you know, when you first said that the house you were renting belonged to a widow who'd moved away. I pictured an old lady who'd gone to live in a nursing home."

"Yeah." Manny laughed with him. "I had that idea, too. That she was some old lady."

"Now, instead of just some old lady you get to make her your old lady … marry her, no?"

Manny's heart thundered to a stop and he raised his eyebrows at his friend.

Diego shrugged. "Why look so surprised? You want to be with her … where else would this be leading?"

It was true. He did want to be with Nina. He didn't know her well enough yet, but he had been thinking of a future between them. But after he'd failed at marriage the first time around, it wasn't something that he'd even considered he would want to try again.

Diego gave his shoulder a shake. "Think about it. But for now, you'd better get going. Especially if you want to catch Don before he leaves work."

Manny had told Diego about what had happened to Nina up in Stanton Falls and that he'd been talking to the sheriff about it. "Okay. I'll see you."

"You will." Diego grinned. "If you don't call me, I'll call you … soon."

It was ten till five when Manny pulled up in the parking lot beside the sheriff's office. He'd intended to get here earlier. He knew these small-town guys were usually keen to get home on a Friday afternoon.

He hoped that Don would make the time to talk with him and not be in too much of a hurry to get out of here.

He needn't have worried. As soon as he got through the door, Colt, the deputy he'd worked most closely with on Zack's case, greeted him with a grim smile.

"Hey, Manny. What do you think? Do you think he'll show his face here?"

Manny frowned. He couldn't know for certain who Colt was talking about, but his instincts told him who it was. And judging by the cold sense of dread and fury that swept through him, he believed that he would come to Summer Lake. "What have you heard?"

"Only what Nina told Don when she called just now. That this Brian guy was in the store where she used to work asking after her. That her colleague didn't know there was a problem and told him that she moved back here."

Manny's hands balled into fists at his sides. He could feel the muscle in his jaw twitch as he clenched his teeth together. He'd fucking kill him before he ever laid another finger on Nina.

Colt took a step back with a wry look on his face. "Damn! Remind me never to cross you? I heard that you …"

"What?" Manny barked out the question before he managed to reel himself in. He forced himself to breathe deeply and to soften his stance and his expression before he spoke again. "Sorry, Colt, what have you heard?"

"That you and Nina … that you … have a special interest there." He gave Manny a half smile. "And judging by your reaction, I think I might have to upgrade that to a very special interest. It's not just because you're staying at her house, right?"

Manny gave him a rueful smile. "I wouldn't lie to you."

"I wouldn't believe you if you did. Your reaction there said it all. It also tells me that Don and I don't have much to worry about."

Manny raised an eyebrow.

"Whatever security and protection she needs, she has you."

"She does." It made him smile again. It was true. He'd protect her from anything, any threat. Not just this dick, Brian.

Colt smiled back at him. "Do you want to come through and see Don? Tell us how we can assist?"

He had to laugh at that. It was an ongoing bone of contention between bureau guys and local law enforcement officers everywhere that the FBI tended to come in and ride roughshod over the locals, taking charge and only giving the local guys basic support duties.

Manny didn't work that way. It wasn't in his nature to be an asshole—not just for the sake of it. He knew he could come across that way when he was focused on getting things done, but he didn't get off on power trips. He'd established a good working relationship with the Lake County sheriff's office when he came up to help Zack out and he knew that he could count on their support now—even though he wasn't here in any official capacity anymore.

Nina lifted the lid on the pan and sniffed. It smelled wonderful, even if she did say so herself. Manny had texted a little while ago to say that he was on his way back. She couldn't help again comparing him to Paul and all the times she used to have to call him to see when he'd be home. It was never when he'd said, and often, when she called, he'd tell her that his plans had changed—that he had to stay over wherever he was working. Now, she knew that he'd stayed at Lorraine's apartment—the one that her swimming pool money had gone to help pay for.

She wiped her hands on her apron before she took it off. She didn't need to be thinking about that. What she should be doing was looking forward to her evening with Manny. A little shiver ran through her at the memory of what he'd said last night about romancing her all evening … and *loving* her all night.

She closed her eyes as the butterflies took to flight again in her stomach and a wave of shivery anticipation rushed through her.

When she opened them again, her smile faded. She was going to have to tell him about Janet's phone call, too. Yes,

Manny made her feel better just by being around, but she didn't want the shadow of Brian or what he'd done to her to hang over their evening. She hated the thought that Manny might feel responsible for her safety. He was supposed to be retired from all that.

She looked up when she heard the front door open. Maybe she shouldn't tell him about it until tomorrow.

Her heart raced when he appeared in the doorway to the kitchen. He was so handsome. Well, he maybe wasn't classically handsome; he had too many hard edges to be that. But there was no denying that he was attractive. There was something powerful—magnetic—about him. Perhaps it was the contrast between the way he looked so harsh and yet his eyes were so kind.

Those eyes were watching her closely as he leaned against the doorframe and folded his arms across his chest.

"Hi."

"Hey. How was your day?"

She hesitated. There was something off with him. He was smiling, but there was an edge to him that she wasn't used to. "It was good, thanks. How was yours?" Now, she sounded off, too. She could be making polite conversation with a stranger and that wasn't how she wanted this evening to go.

He frowned, making her heart sink. Had he changed his mind?

"Do you want to tell me about it?"

She met his gaze, not sure what he meant. At least, she wasn't sure until she looked into his big brown eyes. They told her that he knew. She didn't know how, but the concern she saw in his eyes, and the edge of—anger?—made her feel that he knew about Brian somehow and he was waiting to see if she'd tell him.

She nodded. "I heard from Janet today. Apparently, Brian's looking for me and Kerry told him that I live here … not here, my address, but here at the lake."

His lips pressed into a thin line. There was no mistaking the anger on his face, and this time his frown did make her feel a little intimidated.

"I'm sorry." It was hardly her fault, but somehow, she felt as if it were. That she'd somehow put him in a bad position. She clasped her hands together. This was so not how she'd hoped this evening might go.

He pushed away from the door and came to her. She could see a little pulse working in his jaw.

"Come here." It sounded like a command—one she couldn't disobey even if she'd wanted to. But she didn't want to. She wanted nothing more than to go to him. He closed his arms around her and rested his chin on top of her head. She could feel his heart thundering in his chest. He held her that way for a long few moments before she dared to look up at him.

"I'm sorry," she said again.

His arm tightened around her, and he brushed his lips over hers. "What for? You have nothing to be sorry for, Nina." His voice sounded harsh.

"I know, but … you don't seem very happy. You seem angry. I don't want to land you in the middle of something that you don't need. I don't want to be a damsel in distress who you feel you have to take care of, just when you're supposed to be free of all that."

He closed his eyes and exhaled deeply.

She pulled away. It felt as though he was exasperated, and she didn't want him to feel that way. Didn't want him to have to …

Instead of letting her go, he held her closer to him. She didn't struggle. She didn't want to. She looked up into his eyes and waited to hear what he had to say.

"I thought you understood me, but it seems I'm going to have to explain to make myself clear."

She nodded. She didn't want to hear that he wasn't interested in taking on another case, didn't want to know that he didn't need a damsel in distress, but …

"I'm not very happy. You have that right."

Her heart sank.

"In fact, I'm more than unhappy. I madder than hell that you find yourself in this situation. Yes. I'm supposed to be retired from all of this, but what you don't seem to understand is that I *need* to be in the middle of it. There's nowhere else I'd rather be than right here, with you, protecting you, making sure that you're going to be okay. I need you to be okay because I need you to be with me." He hesitated and looked deep into her eyes. "I believe that we have a future ahead of us, you and me. And I am not going to let anyone fuck with it. I'll rip this bastard limb from limb if he tries to get anywhere near you. I'm sorry if it seems like I'm angry … it's because I am. But don't for one minute think I'm angry at you. I'm angry that anything—anyone—could ever threaten you. But, believe me, he won't ever hurt you."

Her heart was pounding as she looked up into his eyes.

"No one will ever hurt you again, Nina. I'll make sure of it. I'm not great at being with a woman. I've never cared enough to try. But I'll learn. I care about you and I intend to make you happy. You can't be happy with that kind of threat hanging over you and I can't be happy until the threat is eliminated."

She didn't know what to say. Didn't know that there was anything she could say to that. All she knew was that she loved what he was telling her. She knew that he could make her happy and she wanted to make him happy, too.

He lowered his head and brushed his lips over hers. "Did I say too much?"

She shook her head and tightened her arms around him. "No. I think you made yourself quite clear."

He gave her a half smile. "And you don't mind? Do you … feel the same way?"

She let out a big breath and let herself lean against him. "I do. I care about you, too. I'd like to learn how to make you happy."

His face was transformed when he smiled. "You have nothing to learn, just be you. You're what I want."

She reached up and pressed a kiss against his lips. "You're what I want, too."

Chapter Twelve

Manny poured two glasses of wine while Nina served the dessert. He was mad at himself. He should have kept a lid on it. He should have just come in and told her that he knew about Brian. Instead, he'd been a fool. He'd fumed all the way back from the sheriff's office. He'd wanted to smash something when Colt and Don had told him about Nina's call. When he'd spoken to them earlier in the week they'd seemed convinced that the guy was harmless and that Nina wouldn't have any more trouble with him—that out of sight would be out of mind—and, since she was now back here in Summer Lake, she should have heard the last of him.

He'd only gone by today to make sure there was nothing else on him. But instead of reassuring him that this Brian had slunk back into whatever hole he'd crawled out of, they'd told him that Nina had called in a little while ago to let them know what Janet had told her.

She turned around with two dishes in her hands and a hesitant smile. "Do you want to eat this outside?"

He nodded and opened the door for her before following her with the wine. He needed to pull himself together. She was still wary of him and that was all wrong. Tonight was supposed to be about relaxing together, getting to know each other better—in every sense. She already had one asshole who was making her edgy. She didn't need Manny behaving like another one.

He smiled as he sat down beside her at the patio table, then he scooted his chair a little closer and planted a kiss on her forehead.

"Dinner was wonderful, thank you."

She smiled. "I'm glad you enjoyed it. I hope you'll like this, too."

He looked down at the bowl with a little chocolate cake and two scoops of ice cream.

She must have read his mind. She nudged him with her elbow. "I guessed that you might not have much of a sweet tooth, so it's salted caramel ice cream and bitter chocolate."

He had to laugh and couldn't resist nudging her back. "Are you trying to tell me that I'm not sweet? That I am, in fact, bitter and salty?"

She laughed with him. "The thought hadn't even occurred to me, but now that you mention it . . ."

He drew his eyebrows together in a frown that he knew daunted most people, but she just laughed.

"Don't give me that look. You don't scare me!"

A rush of warmth filled his chest at her words; that was what he needed to know. Earlier, when he'd first come in, it'd seemed as though she maybe was scared of him, and that killed him.

He set his spoon down and cupped his hand around the back of her neck, brushing his thumb over her nape. "Say that again."

Her smile faded. "What?"

"You know."

"You don't scare me."

He held her gaze, wanting her to know how important that was, but not wanting to say the words.

His heart clenched in his chest when she leaned in and planted a peck on his lips. "You don't. You probably should, but … you make me feel safe. That's probably the only thing that scares me. I don't want you to see me as someone you need to rescue."

"I don't." He shook his head determinedly. "Nope. It's not that. I don't want to rescue you. I do want to take care of you. I want to protect you, but not because I see you as weak or needy."

"Why then?" She looked into his eyes and he had to tell her the truth.

"Because I see you as mine."

Her eyes widened. He shouldn't have said it, but he couldn't take it back. He didn't want to. It was the truth.

She reached both hands up and cupped his face between them. His heart pounded faster as he wondered if she was about to tell him that she wasn't his, that she never would be.

"I'm not yours, Manny."

He nodded sadly and started to pull away, but she kept hold of his face and made him look at her.

"Not yet," she added.

Hope soared in his chest again. "You think you might be someday?"

A smile twitched on her lips, and she nodded. Then she got to her feet and took hold of his hand. He stood and gave her a puzzled look. "Where are we going?"

Her cheeks flamed bright red, but she met his gaze. "Upstairs, if you want to make me yours."

Wow! He hadn't expected that. But he wanted it; he wanted her—so badly it ached. "Are you sure?"

She nodded, her cheeks still red. "I am, but saying that took everything I had. I can't ask you again. Don't make me."

He closed his arms around her and held her to his chest as he covered her mouth with his and kissed her deeply.

When she looked up at him, her eyes shone, and she was breathing hard. Her body gave him the answer, but he needed to hear her say it. "Do you want to make love to me, Nina? I need you to be sure. For your sake and for mine. I can wait. But I don't think I can take you and make you mine and then watch you walk away."

She trembled in his arms. "I'm not a walk away kind of girl. When I'm in, I'm all in."

"For keeps?" What the hell was he doing? He shouldn't be asking so many questions. He should just take her at her word and take her to bed. But he had to know. It might be too fast, too soon. But he knew in his gut that she could be it for him.

She could be his future if she wanted to be. But she needed to be sure.

"For as long as you want me."

He pressed a kiss to her lips and repeated. "For keeps."

Nina's heart thundered in her chest as she let him lead her upstairs. He must be able to feel how sweaty her palm was. He must know how nervous she was. She felt as though she was about to have sex for the very first time. At her age, that was ridiculous, but at the same time, it was kind of true. It would be the first time with anyone other than Paul. She watched Manny's broad back and muscular thighs as he went up the stairs ahead of her. He was nothing like Paul!

He stopped when he reached the landing and squeezed her hand. "Where?"

She laughed. It was good to release a little of the tension. "I think in bed … this first time, at least."

He chuckled and shook his head at her. "I didn't mean that, though now I'll be thinking about other, less conventional places."

A rush of heat coursed through her and settled between her legs when he said that and let his gaze run over her.

"I meant, which room."

"Oh." She should be pleased that he was aware enough to consider that she might not want to sleep with him in the bedroom that she'd shared with Paul. But at the same time, she wished she didn't have to think about that.

She smiled as a thought stuck her and she tugged his hand, taking him to her room—Abbie's room. She was glad she'd moved into it since she came back. She might still be living in her old home, but she hadn't fallen back into being the same person.

He followed her and closed the door behind him then leaned back against it and folded his arms across his chest.

She'd kind of hoped that he might take charge and undress her or throw her on the bed or do something—anything—other than stand there staring at her like that.

"Come here."

Oh! Now, that … She felt her feet obey him even as the rest of her quivered in anticipation.

When she reached him, he closed his arms around her, and she smiled up at him.

"I take it you're not only used to being in charge but that you enjoy it?"

The corners of his lips quirked up in the hint of a smile. "I guess you could say that. I'm sorry. That wasn't meant to be an order. I'm trying here, trying to keep my cool."

He closed his hands around her ass and held her against him. His hard-on pressed into her belly, making her suck in a deep breath at the feel of him.

She slipped her hands under the hem of his T-shirt and stroked them up over his chest, loving the way his eyelids drooped and his hands tightened around her ass. "I think I'd like to see you lose your cool."

His eyes opened and the desire that burned in them made her heart race. "I have no doubt that you will, but not this first time."

She bit down on her bottom lip and nodded. "Please? I know all about mechanical sex. Dutiful sex. Routine sex. I don't know what it's like to make a man lose his cool."

"And you want to?"

She nodded again. She wanted nothing more than for him to take her because he couldn't resist her. She didn't need gentle and she didn't want slow. She wanted him to make her his, just like he'd said.

He held her gaze as he brushed his thumb over her lips and rocked his hips against her. She let out a little moan and couldn't resist licking his thumb and taking it inside her mouth.

His eyes burned with intensity as he watched. Then he pulled it out and trailed it down between her breasts. She closed her eyes when his hand kept moving lower and lower. He lifted her skirt and slid his hand inside her panties, making her moan when his thumb that was still wet from her mouth started to circle her clit.

He pressed his flattened palm against her as he worked her and claimed her mouth in a kiss that felt like a precursor of what was to come. He buried his other hand in her hair and pulled her head back, giving him better access and opening her up to allow his tongue to sweep deeper.

She'd never been kissed like that in her life, but she could barely focus on it. His thumb was still tormenting her clit in rhythmic movements. Now his finger was resting at her entrance and she tensed, knowing that at any moment he was going to ... oh, God! She moaned into his mouth when he pushed deep and set up a relentless rhythm.

She clung to his shoulders and kissed him back. He was going to make her come right here as they stood against the door and there was nothing she wanted more. She rocked her hips in time with his movements, and then he thrust deeper and touched her in a place that made stars explode behind her eyes. She moaned her way through the best orgasm she'd had in years.

When she finally stilled, she rested her head against his shoulder—embarrassed to look up into his eyes.

"Good?"

She nodded, but still didn't look up.

He tucked his fingers under her chin and made her look at him. "Not good?" He raised an eyebrow.

"Very, very good," she breathed.

"But?"

"There's no hiding anything from you, is there?"

He chuckled and dropped a kiss on her lips. "I'm afraid not. So, tell me what's bothering you."

"I wanted it to be about you, too."

The way he smiled made her nipples tighten and little aftershocks shivered through her. "It was. You said you want me to take you. I'm going to. This was just a little warm-up to make sure that you're good and ready for me first."

His words and the way he spoke them had her back at the edge. She felt as though she'd been petting a pony and only just now realized that he was a wild stallion.

He pulled his shirt up and off revealing a lean muscular chest that she couldn't resist running her fingers over.

His eyes burned into hers when he led her toward the bed. He sat down and tugged her hand so that she sat on his lap. "I'm going to give you one more chance to back out." His voice was husky when he spoke.

"I don't want to."

He nodded and claimed her mouth in a kiss that made her head spin. His lips never left hers, yet within moments she was lying there naked. He lifted his head and let his gaze travel over her while he pushed down his jeans and boxers.

Nina let her gaze rove over him, too. His body was hard, his shoulders broad and muscular. His chest and abs well defined and … she sucked in a deep breath as her gaze continued lower… wow. She didn't want to get caught up in the past. She wanted to be right here in this moment with Manny. But she couldn't help comparing; Paul hadn't been quite the man Manny was.

He lay down beside her and stroked his fingers over her cheek. "You're beautiful."

She smiled. "I'm not bad for an old bird." She couldn't resist running her fingers over his chest. "You're beautiful."

He caught her hand and brought it up to kiss her fingers, then he took them one at a time into his mouth. The way he swirled his tongue over her fingertips had her wriggling with need for him.

He brought her hand down trailing it over his chest and stomach and then placed it over his erection.

He was so hard and hot. She curled her fingers around him, loving the way he sucked in a sharp breath and twitched in her hand.

His hand closed around the back of her neck. "Do you want that?"

She nodded breathlessly. She didn't think she'd ever wanted anything more.

His arm closed around her, crushing her to his chest as he kissed her again. His hand wandered over her, burning a trail into her skin. His fingers found their way between her legs again and she parted them to give him better access.

Then he positioned himself above her, propping himself up on his elbows to look down into her eyes. She could feel him pulsating at her entrance. She needed to feel him inside her.

"Please, Manny." She'd beg if she needed to. She was desperate now for him to … "Oh, God, yes!"

He thrust deep and hard, stretching her, filling her. Her mind spun away as he struck up a punishing rhythm. He felt so hard, so right as he drove deep inside her over and over again.

He felt so damned good, she never wanted it to end, but then he slowed. She looked up at him in a panic when he pulled out. He hadn't? He couldn't leave her high and dry like that?

He gave her a knowing smile as he got to his knees and breathed. "More."

He hooked his arms behind her knees and wrapped her legs around his waist when he thrust deep inside her once again.

"Manny!" she gasped. He was deeper and harder even than before. One hand grasped her hip, the other moved over her, teasing her nipples and making her moan. Then he found her clit again and rolled it between his finger and thumb. Her back arched up off the bed and his thrusts became more frantic.

He was pushing her over the edge and all she could do was let go. "Oh, oh, Manny! Yesss!"

As her orgasm took her, she felt him tense and his next thrust felt as though it lodged him deep inside her as he came hard.

Waves of pleasure racked her body. Her muscles fluttered, clenching him tight as if they were trying to make him part of her.

When they lay still and he looked into her eyes, she knew that in some way, she had. When he rolled to the side to wrap her up in his arms, he came out of her, but the connection that they now shared went beyond the physical.

She looked up at him, wondering if he felt it too. His eyes were serious as he dropped a kiss on the tip of her nose.

"You said it was what you wanted."

She smiled. "It was so much better than what I wanted."

"It was amazing, but I didn't mean that."

"What then?"

"You said you wanted me to make you mine. Now you are."

Her heart felt as though it melted in her chest. All she'd wanted in her marriage was to feel like Paul saw her as his partner, his friend even. She'd given up on hoping that he'd see her as a woman many years ago. She'd felt as though they were at least a team … until she'd found out about Lorraine and then she'd discovered that all he'd seen her as was a hindrance to getting what he really wanted in life.

Now, Manny was saying that she was what he wanted. He could have anything, go anywhere, she knew that. He could no doubt have any woman he wanted too. But he was here in her bed. He'd just made love to her and now he was telling her that she was his.

She tightened her arms around him and landed a kiss on his lips. "I am. I'm yours and …" She hesitated to say it. In her experience, men didn't like to feel tied down and obligated. But she had to say it anyway. "And you're mine."

The way he smiled made her glad she hadn't held back.

"I am. All yours. Only yours." He nipped her bottom lip playfully, and his hand came up to cup her breast. "For as long and as often as you want me."

She chuckled. "You want more?"

He ducked his head and nipped her neck. "I want of all of you."

"You've got me."

His arm tightened around her and she relaxed against him. "And I plan to keep you.

Chapter Thirteen

It took Nina a few moments to figure out where she was when she woke up. She'd gotten used to waking up here in Abbie's room, but something was different this morning. A smile spread across her face when she remembered what it was … Manny.

His arm was curled around her waist, his head rested on her shoulder. She could feel the hard muscles of his chest warm against her back. She snuggled against him and closed her eyes again, wanting to enjoy the moment.

"Are you awake?"

She smiled. "No."

He chuckled and planted a kiss in her hair. "You need more sleep?"

"No, but I think I might be dreaming and I'm enjoying it. I don't want to wake up and have it be over."

"What are you dreaming?"

"That there's a wonderful man in bed with me. A man who likes me and wants to be with me."

"That's reality, Nina."

She turned and looked over her shoulder at him. "No regrets?"

His eyebrows drew together. "Not a one. You?"

She shook her head. "Nope. I'm happy."

"Good. That's the plan."

"The plan?"

"To make you happy."

She turned over and looked up into his eyes. "Do you think I can make you happy?"

He brushed his thumb over her lips. "You do."

She wanted to explain that she meant going forward. He'd said some things that implied that he wanted this to be a relationship—that he saw a future with her. But still. They'd only known each other a week. She wanted to believe that when he talked about her being his, he meant long term, but she knew that it could be short lived. He could still decide to leave at the end of the month. She'd accept it if he did. But her heart ached at the thought.

He was looking deep into her eyes. "I meant what I said last night, Nina. Those weren't just words. I didn't make love to you lightly. That means something to me. I hope it does to you?"

"It does. It means the world to me." She pursed her lips and decided to tell him. "It means more to me than I think you realize."

He frowned and waited.

What the heck. She'd started, so she'd tell him. "That isn't something I do lightly. For me … there's only been Paul."

His eyes widened in surprise. She felt foolish. She didn't want to think about how many women might have shared his bed.

He held her close and dropped a kiss on the top of her head. "Thank you."

She had to laugh.

"What?" He leaned back so he could see her face. "I'm serious. Why is that funny?"

She laughed again. "I don't know. I just don't see sex as something that a person would say thank you for."

He smiled through pursed lips. "It isn't. But that wasn't just sex. We made love. And what I'm saying thank you for is for trusting me and for sharing yourself with me."

She nodded. "I don't know about you, but I'm not one to lie around in bed in the morning." She slipped away from him and got up, pulling her robe around her as she went. Of course, she liked the idea of making love to him again, but she needed a shower, she wanted to brush her teeth before she kissed him again. And she needed coffee.

He chuckled as he got up. "I know what you want. And I didn't have time to set up the coffee pot for you last night. I'll meet you down there."

He came around the bed and landed another kiss on top of her head. She had to admire his hard body—and the way he moved so confidently—totally unfazed by the fact that he was naked. She knew she wasn't in bad shape, but she couldn't see herself strutting around naked in front of him just yet.

He stepped back and looked down at himself, seeming to pick up on her thoughts. He shrugged. "Sorry. I hope you can get used to me and my ways."

She nodded happily. She'd love to.

~ ~ ~

It was early evening by the time they got back to the house. They'd taken a drive up in the mountains. It was cooler up there and Manny had wanted to spend the day alone with her. This morning he'd been concerned that she might back off, become wary after sleeping with him. But he needn't have worried. It had brought them closer. She was more relaxed with him today. She laughed easily and had even started to tease him. He was more hopeful about what the future might hold for them.

He frowned to himself as he followed her inside the house. If she were going to be a part of his future, there were decisions that would need to be made.

He looked around the kitchen. He'd be happy to move here—to Summer Lake—but he had no desire to move into her house. Retirement was going to be a new start for him. He wanted their relationship to start out in a new place, too. He was getting ahead of himself.

First, they needed to take some time to figure out if what they shared would last. Also, he needed to make sure that this Brian character was out of the picture once and for all. He didn't do well with unfinished business. He needed to track the guy down and make sure that he wouldn't ever bother Nina again.

She turned and smiled at him. "That was a wonderful day. Thank you. I should see about fixing us some dinner."

"No."

She raised an eyebrow at him. "No? You're not hungry?"

He went to her and slid his arms around her waist. He couldn't help himself. He wanted to hold her whenever he was close to her. They'd just spent the afternoon in the car together, but he'd only been able to hold her hand.

She didn't seem to mind. She relaxed against him as she smiled up at him. "You don't want to eat?"

"I do. But I don't want you to have to cook. I know you say that you don't mind, but you shouldn't have to."

Her smile faded. "You want to go out to eat?"

"Not if you don't. But we could order takeout from the restaurant."

She thought about it and then nodded slowly. "We could. Or we can eat there if you prefer? I don't want you thinking that all you ever get to do with me is stay home."

He dropped a kiss on her lips. "I don't care either way. What matters is that I'm with you."

She held his gaze for a long moment before she spoke again. "Have you had a lot of women?"

He frowned.

"I didn't mean that the way it sounded. I meant, is this normal for you? Do you start seeing someone, enjoy their company for a while, say all the flowery words and do the things that make her feel good and then … leave her with just a memory?"

He understood what she meant. "Are you thinking that I see you as some kind of vacation fling?"

She hung her head. "Not exactly."

He cupped her cheek in his hand and made her look up at him. "Well, I don't. I'm sorry if I'm being too full-on. Too intense. But that doesn't mean I see this as something that will burn bright and fast and then fizzle out. I've told you how I see it. I know it's too fast. But that's the way I've had to live. That's how my work was, and my work has been my whole life. I'm used to going into a new situation and having to figure out fast how it will pan out. I've learned to trust my instincts and act on them. My instincts tell me that you're the one for me."

Her eyes widened, but she smiled.

"I'll play this any way you want to. But you should know that I'm not just having fun here. I'm all in with you."

She searched his face for a moment and then nodded. "Let's go out for dinner then."

He raised an eyebrow, not understanding her change of mind.

"If we're going to be together, we'll need to figure out what our normal is going to be. You already know what it's like to hang out here at the house with me. I don't know what it's like to go out and be with you in public. But I'd like to find out. I keep second-guessing myself that you're going to change your mind any minute. But I have to stop that. I have to take you at your word and believe all the wonderful things you're telling me. So, I don't want to hide out at home. I want to step into something new with you … and let people see that we're together."

He dropped a kiss on her lips. "Only if it's what you want."

"It is." She looked happier than he'd seen her before when she smiled. "I've been a homebody for so long that I don't remember now if it's by choice or just by habit. I think it'll be fun to go out with you."

"I'll make sure it is."

Nina took a deep breath when Manny held the door to the restaurant open for her. She'd told him that she wanted to come out and that she didn't mind people seeing that they were together. It was true, but she was a little nervous. She'd lived here all her life. She knew almost everyone in this town, but they knew her as a married woman. She was part of Paul and Nina. She was Abbie's mom. She had to wonder what people would think when they saw her with Manny.

He put his arm around her shoulders and started walking toward the bar. "Do you want to get a quiet table somewhere?"

She chuckled. "No, thank you. I don't. I don't do half measures. We're here; I'd like to enjoy it."

He smiled down at her. "You tell me then. Do you want to have dinner with Diego and Ted?" He jerked his head to where his friends were sitting with Audrey and Izzy. "Would you rather get a booth and eat by ourselves and then hang out with them later? Or …" She followed his gaze and her heart raced when she saw Ivan and Abbie coming toward them. "Do you want to catch up with your daughter first, and we can decide from there?"

She smiled at Abbie who was eyeing Manny's arm around her shoulders. This should prove interesting. "I guess we're about to find out what Abbie has to say, and then I think I'll need a drink."

"Hi, Mom. I didn't know you were coming out tonight." Abbie greeted her with a smile and then turned to Manny. "You've done well to get her out. It's nice to see you."

"It's nice to see you, too. I managed to persuade your mom that we could eat out."

She could tell that Abbie liked hearing that. "Good for you. I'm surprised at you though, Mom. I didn't think it was possible to drag you away from the kitchen on a Saturday night."

Nina smiled at her. "Neither did I. But Manny made it easy." She smiled up at him. She wanted him to know that she was glad she'd come. And she wanted Abbie to see that she was glad to be here with him.

"That earns you brownie points in my book, Manny," said Ivan.

Nina watched the smile the two men exchanged. She hadn't thought they knew each other, but they seemed to.

"Are you meeting up with friends?" asked Abbie.

Nina shrugged. "We're going to have dinner and play it by ear. Are you meeting up with the gang?"

"Yep. Everyone's outside."

"And we should get out there," said Ivan.

Nina guessed that he was trying to make things easy for them, and she appreciated it.

"Yeah. Come and find us later if you like," said Abbie.

"We might."

They watched them go and join their friends out on the deck where the band had set up on a little stage.

Manny's arm tightened around her shoulders. "How do you feel about that?" he asked as he steered her toward the bar.

She smiled. "It feels good. I should be honest and tell you that Abbie thinks you're wonderful.

She loved the way he smiled at that. "She does?"

"Yes. It seems that most—if not all—of the girls do."

He frowned, and she realized what he must be thinking.

"I didn't mean anything by that. I know that if you wanted a hot young thing you'd go and be with one."

It was a good thing that she was already used to his facial expressions. If she didn't know better, she'd think he was angry at her. "I'm glad you know it. I wasn't looking for anything, for anyone. I'm with you because you took me by surprise and bowled me over. If I'm not with you, then I'm not going to be with anyone." He was deadly serious. He wasn't just saying it to reassure her. He was telling the truth.

She rested her head against his shoulder. "It's the same for me."

"Is it?" This time his scowl looked more convincing.

"Yes. Why?"

He shook his head and she knew he was going to clam up on her. She ducked out from under his arm. "Tell me the truth."

He blew out a sigh. "I'm sorry. But weren't you dating?"

"Oh! No. Not really. That was Janet's idea. I went out with Brian because she thought it would do me good. Not because I was looking for someone."

"I know. I'm sorry. I don't mean to be an asshole. It's just when I think about him ... I get angry."

"Well, don't think about him then. Don't let him ruin our evening." She linked her arm through his and led him the rest of the way to the bar. "Let's a get a drink and have dinner, and then I might have to make you dance with me."

The corners of his lips twitched up in the hint of a smile. "Okay."

~ ~ ~

Manny smiled to himself as he watched her chatting and laughing with the other women. Marianne and Chris had joined Izzy and Audrey and the five of them were having a ball. He was fascinated to watch her interact with them. She said she didn't socialize much, but she seemed to be enjoying it. Audrey and Marianne were both quieter, while Izzy and Chris were more outgoing. Nina was definitely on the outgoing side. She and Izzy seemed to share the same sense of humor and he'd guess that she already knew Chris well.

He smiled when Diego's hand came down on his shoulder. "I thought you said she wasn't someone who liked to be part of a group. It seems to me that she's the life of the party. Were you just trying to keep her all to yourself?"

"No." Manny turned to look at him. "I think the Nina we're seeing tonight is who she really is, but who she'd forgotten she was."

Diego nodded. "And you're going to remind her?"

"I hope to support her while she figures it out for herself."

"And I always thought you didn't have a heart."

He laughed at Ted who had come to stand on his other side. "That's not true. You've always known that I simply kept it well hidden."

"Yeah. I hope you're going to follow it with Nina? I have high hopes."

"Me too. I …" He stopped mid-sentence when he spotted a very familiar face on the other side of the deck.

"What is it?" asked Diego.

"It's okay. I've just seen someone I haven't run into in years."

"Who?"

He shook his head. He didn't want to say because he didn't know what name he might be going by these days … or why he was here in Summer Lake.

"Give me a minute, guys?"

Ted and Diego nodded. He looked at Nina. He hated to interrupt her conversation, but he decided that was preferable to her not being able to find him and wondering where he'd gone.

He went and stood closer to the girls, waiting for Chris to finish speaking before he put a hand on Nina's shoulder.

Her eyes shone when she turned to look up at him. She looked happy and relaxed, he wanted to be the reason she looked that way all the time.

"Are you okay?"

"I'm fine. I just wanted to let you know that I'm going over there. He pointed to the other side of the deck. I've spotted someone I haven't talked to in years and I'd like to catch up with him."

"Okay." Her hand came up to cover his and even though she didn't speak the words, her eyes thanked him for coming to let her know. He couldn't help but think that her husband would have just gone without giving her a second thought.

"Aww!" He had to laugh when Izzy grinned at him. "I had you down as a real tough nut. But you're just a big pussy cat, aren't you?"

He shrugged and looked down at Nina. "For some reason I seem to have discovered my softer side, lately." He knew he shouldn't, but he had to. He dropped a kiss on her lips and then turned on his heel and walked away.

He smiled at Dan Benson when he reached the group on the other side of the deck. He'd chatted with Dan a few times and planned to talk with him again soon. He'd set up a cybersecurity operation here and Manny wouldn't mind doing some freelancing with him in the future.

Dan turned to get his friend's attention, but Manny shook his head. He'd take great pleasure in being able to take Ryan Brady by surprise.

He waited until he was right behind him before he spoke. "Cocky. Insidious. Asshole."

Ryan spun around and laughed when he saw Manny. "Damn! You got me! What the fuck are you doing here, Famous But Incompetent?"

Manny laughed with him. "Me? I'm retired. Just visiting to see if I can settle into living the small-town life."

"Seriously?"

"Yeah. And I think I've already figured out that I can."

"Well, I'll be damned. So, we're going to be neighbors?"

"What?"

Ryan grinned. "Yeah. I'm not so ancient and decrepit as you are, old man. But … I'm out. I'm going to be helping Danny boy here."

Dan nodded. He didn't tend to say too much, but it was worth listening when he did. Manny narrowed his eyes when a thought occurred him. Jibing with Ryan as he always had about their respective agencies' acronyms had him making a connection about Dan's work that hadn't occurred to him before.

Dan grinned at him and his eyes twinkled when he said. "Before you ask, I should warn you, I'm Not Saying Anything."

Manny laughed out loud. "Well I'll be damned. Why didn't I see it?"

Ryan jabbed his arm. "Because you're past it, old man."

Manny's arm shot out and he caught Ryan's wrist. "Don't you believe it. I'm retired because that's the age they set. They have to account for the norm – you know I've never been the norm."

Ryan laughed and pulled his arm free. "No, you never have. I don't normally have time for any of you Bureau guys. You're the only one who ever earned my respect. In fact …" He shot a look at Dan. "I'd be honored to work with you, if the occasion arises."

Manny met Dan's gaze, and he smiled. "I'd say the occasion probably will if you're interested. We should get together sometime before you leave."

"Whenever you like." Manny grinned. "I'm not leaving."

Chapter Fourteen

Nina went in the back office to collect her purse. She was supposed to get out of here at five, but so far it hadn't worked out that way. It was five-twenty on Thursday afternoon, and this was the earliest she'd managed to leave this week.

Joanne gave her an apologetic smile as she made her way out. "Sorry, Nina. I'll see you tomorrow. And I promise we'll get you out of here at five if not before."

She waved a hand at the younger woman. "Don't worry about it. It's not a problem."

Joanne waggled her eyebrows. "It'll be Friday night. Are you going to tell me you don't have a hot date with the delicious Manny Alvarado?"

Nina rolled her eyes. It seemed that she and Manny were the subject of much gossip around town since they'd been seen out together last weekend. Manny had done nothing but fuel the rumors by the way he'd danced with her … and kissed her on the dance floor before they left. But all she'd done all week was smile politely and say nothing. So, she wasn't about to tell Joanne that there'd be nothing special about Friday night; at least, no more special than every other night. She and Manny had dinner together, went for walks or just hung out at the house … and made love.

Joanne laughed. "I know you're not going to say anything, but your face says it all. I don't blame you. But I do envy you."

Nina laughed. It seemed that every single woman and a few of the married ones, no matter how old or young they were, would love to be in her shoes—or more accurately, in Manny's bed.

"I'll see you tomorrow."

She was almost to the front door when she stopped. A shiver ran down her spine and she glanced over at the rack of T-shirts. A man was browsing through them. She let out the breath she didn't know she'd been holding when he turned and smiled at her. For a moment there she'd been convinced it was Brian.

"Do you have these in other sizes?"

"Sorry, only what's on display in those designs. They're leftovers from last year."

"Okay, thanks."

He looked so disappointed she couldn't help it. She went over to him. "What are you looking for?"

He held up a red women's V-neck T-shirt that said *The Lake is My Happy Place.* "I wondered if you had this in a 2XL. My sister couldn't make it up here this year and I wanted to take her one back. She always says the lake is her happy place and she's missing out this time."

Nina rifled through the shirts on the rack, she knew they'd had some 2XLs and she didn't remember selling any.

"Here." She grinned when she got to them. "There isn't a red one, but we have blue, black, green, and white."

The guy smiled back at her. "Thanks! I'll get her a green one."

He took the shirt from her and made his way to the cash register.

Nina hitched the strap of her purse higher on her shoulder and started toward the door. This time, she stopped dead when she saw Manny standing just inside it with his arms folded across his chest.

He smiled, and she pulled herself together and hurried to him. "This is a nice surprise. What are you doing here?"

He dropped a kiss on her lips, and she couldn't help shooting a sideways glance at Joanne, knowing that the grapevine would be buzzing as soon as they left here.

Manny straightened up with a frown and led her outside. "I'm sorry," he said once were they were out in the warm sunshine.

"What for?"

"I didn't think. I shouldn't have come into your work and kissed you like that."

She smiled up at him. "Why not? I'm not sorry. I liked it."

He raised an eyebrow. "But you were wary of what your co-worker will think."

She let out a little laugh. "Nothing gets by you, does it?"

He shook his head solemnly. "Not a thing."

"Okay. Well, if you must know, I wasn't worried what she'd think. I already know. She's jealous. I've done my best all week not to say anything much about us. But just before you came in, she was teasing me about making sure I get out of here on time tomorrow because I no doubt have a hot date."

He smiled and curled his arm around her as they started walking across the square. "You do, if you want one."

She chuckled. "I've had one every night this week, but I wasn't about to tell Joanne that."

He closed his fingers around the back of her neck, a move that he'd discovered turned her on. She narrowed her eyes at him. "I thought you were only going to do that when we were behind closed doors."

He chuckled. "Sorry, I forgot. But since you mention it, are you ready to go home?"

She nodded. She'd wondered when he'd shown up at the store if perhaps, he'd come out so that they could have dinner at the resort. They'd said they might tonight.

His thumb brushed over her nape. "If you're hungry we can eat now, but when you mention closed doors, I want to take you behind one. We can come back out afterward to eat."

"I like the sound of that." She loved the sound of it. Her life had never been like this and she was loving it. Manny was making it clear in everything he said and did that he wanted to be with her. He loved being in bed with her and had the stamina to keep proving it. But he didn't make her feel like that was all he wanted.

"What about your car?"

Her hand came up to cover her mouth. "Oops. It's around the back of the store. It's not my fault though, I can't focus on practical details when you show up and kiss me. Everything else goes out of my head."

The lines around his eyes crinkled as he smiled down at her. "Do you need it? I'll bring you to work in the morning if you like."

She didn't even need to think about it. She'd much rather go straight home with him than waste time going back for her car. "Let's go. I can bring it home later if we come out to eat."

Manny opened his eyes and instinctively curled his arm tighter around Nina's waist. He did it every morning. He couldn't help it. His first conscious thoughts for years had been to do a quick rundown of where he was and why he was there. For the last week, that rundown had filled him with surprise verging on disbelief and undeniable happiness when he registered that he was here, in Summer Lake, in Nina's bed and that she was right there in his arms.

She gave a little murmur and snuggled closer against him, waking his cock. But no. Much as he would like to start the day that way, it wouldn't be fair. He could spend all morning making love to her if he liked … well, he would like. But she couldn't. She had to get up and go to work. She claimed to enjoy it. From what he'd seen the few times he'd been into the store she was good at it. But he wished she didn't have to go. It wasn't about him being selfish—not completely. Of course, he'd love to spend lazy mornings in bed with her and spend all day hanging out with her. But, more than that, he hated that she had to go, that she needed the money.

He pursed his lips as he hugged her closer to his chest. There was nothing he could do about it. Not yet. It was another item on the list of issues that he was keeping to himself for now, but that they'd have to address before they could move forward together. To his mind that meant that he'd have to address them soon because he wanted nothing more than for the two of them to move forward—to start a life together.

She turned and looked up at him over her shoulder with sleepy eyes. "Morning."

He pressed a kiss into her hair. "Good morning, beautiful."

She made a face. "I'm hardly that. Especially when I first wake up. I know my hair's like a bird's nest and my eyes are puffy."

He kissed first one eyelid and then the other and chuckled as he tangled his fingers in her tousled hair. "That's what makes you beautiful."

She laughed. "And I thought you were going to tell me that they're not."

"You know I won't lie to you, Nina. Not even to flatter you. You're beautiful with sleepy eyes and messy hair. You're beautiful with your makeup on and your hair all done. To me, you're just beautiful. Inside, outside, and upside down."

She laughed. "Upside down? Is that your way of hinting that it's time we get more adventurous?"

He raised an eyebrow and then laughed with her when he understood what she meant. "It wasn't, but I wouldn't say no."

She gave him a coy smile. "You know I have to get up now, but maybe tonight?"

His cock strained at the thought of it. "Like I said, I wouldn't say no."

He watched her roll out of bed. He'd already learned that her abrupt exits were to cover her embarrassment. Much as he liked her suggestion, he didn't want to make her feel uncomfortable. He got up and caught her before she went into the bathroom. "I don't need it, though. I love what we have."

She looked up into his eyes. "I know you do. I do, too. I think I'd like to get more adventurous … not only in that way, but in life. I'm just not sure if I'm ready to yet."

"You'll figure out what you want as we go. I'm in for as much or as little adventure as you want to share with me."

"Thanks, Manny."

He closed his arms around her but only for a moment. She needed to get in the shower, and he already knew that he was in danger of never letting her go.

"You can drop me off in front of the store," Nina said when they reached the square at the resort. "There's no need to go all the way around the back."

He pursed his lips and drove on.

She laughed. "Did you even hear me? I think that's the first time you've completely ignored something I've said. You're normally such a good listener."

He glanced over at her and made himself smile. "I should warn you then. There are some subjects where I get all hardheaded and won't be able to hear anything you say."

Her smile faded. "And what subjects are they?"

He reached across and took hold of her hand as he drove down the alley behind the stores. "The subject of your safety is the main one. I think it's the only one, but I used the plural to give myself some leeway in case any other nonnegotiables crop up."

"My safety? You're taking me into the back alley because my safety is at stake?"

He shrugged, realizing that he shouldn't have brought the matter up, and hoping that she wasn't going to get pissed at him.

"How is it safer to bring me around the back rather than let me in the front? That doesn't even make sense, Manny."

"I want to check on your car since it's been here overnight. And I want to make sure that the coast is clear when you go into work. The front entrance is safer by virtue of the fact that it's out on the square. The back is more likely to pose a problem."

She shook her head. "That makes even less sense. I've been coming in the back way every morning by myself. Parking the car … unlocking the back door. Why is it a problem all of a sudden because my car stayed here last night?"

"It's not."

She frowned. "So why do you think it might be more dangerous this morning?"

"I don't." He wished she'd leave it, but he knew he'd have to tell her the truth if she wouldn't let it go. He couldn't have her thinking that he was only just taking an interest in her safety.

"I don't get it. Why is this morning different?"

"It isn't."

"But you didn't need to see me get inside safely any other morning."

He blew out a sigh. Here it came. "I did."

"What … what do you mean?"

"What I said."

"That you saw me get inside safely some other morning?"

"Every morning."

"Manny?"

He swung the car around and parked it next to hers in the little lot behind the store. He cut the engine and turned to her. "I don't want you to be mad at me."

"I don't know what to think. Please tell me what you mean?"

He shrugged. If she hated him for it then it was probably better that they both find that out now. That didn't stop his heart racing as he second-guessed himself about whether it had been a stupid move in the first place. "I mean that I have …" There was no point in carefully choosing words. It was time for the truth. "I followed you here every morning. And I made sure that you were safe inside before I left."

Her eyes widened in shock. "How? I didn't see you. Not once."

He shrugged again. "Does that surprise you?"

"Given what you used to do, then I suppose not. But, Manny, why?"

"Come on, Nina. Because a guy attacked you just before I met you. Because he knows that you live here at the lake. He might come looking for you. I need to know that you're safe. I have to do everything in my power to make sure that you are."

She stared at him for a long moment. He was starting to think that maybe he'd blown it. Perhaps she now saw him as some weird stalker type. He couldn't blame her if she did. But he couldn't change who he was either.

His heart raced while he waited for her to speak … waited to hear her pass judgment on his actions. Actions that he knew must seem strange.

Relief flooded though him when she smiled and breathed, "Wow!"

He caught hold of her hand. "Wow? Is wow good?" He thought it was, but he needed to hear her say so.

She clasped his hand in both of hers. "Yeah, it's good." She bit down on her bottom lip. "Some little part of my mind thinks that I should probably be more independent, possibly even be offended or upset, but I can't be. I guess I'm old-fashioned at heart, but you doing that … it just tells me that you must care about me."

"Oh, I care, Nina. I care a lot."

He leaned toward her and she met him in the middle for a kiss that was all too short. He was tempted to tell her just how much he cared. It might make his actions more understandable. On the other hand, it might make them seem even more crazy.

Chapter Fifteen

"Are you ready for another?"

A big smile spread across Nina's face, and her chest filled with warmth as she nodded. "Thanks."

Manny raised an eyebrow as he refilled her mug. "What's that look for?"

She tried to seem innocent. "What look?"

There was no fooling Manny—about anything, it seemed. He set the coffee pot back down and came to wrap his arms around her. "You know what I mean. You looked like I'd asked if you wanted the winning lottery ticket. I know you like your coffee, but I don't think that's the reason you look so happy."

She shrugged and buried her face in his chest. "Why shouldn't I be happy? It's Saturday morning. I don't have to go to work. And you just offered me more coffee."

He chuckled and tucked his fingers under her chin, making her look up into his eyes—eyes that were twinkling with amusement, and with something else, something that told her that perhaps he already knew what she was so happy about.

"Tell me."

She shook her head. She wasn't sure that she wanted to admit it. She shouldn't be so thrilled by the offer of a refill.

His eyebrows came together, and he gave her a stern look. "Do I need to interrogate you?"

She had to laugh. "Ooh, maybe. That sounds like it could be fun."

He shook his head with a laugh. "Tell me what you're hiding, and I'll give you all the fun you can handle."

Her body reacted to his words, knowing that he could— and he would. "Well, since you put it like that …" She hesitated. She knew he'd be pleased to hear that his little gestures meant so much to her, but she had to wonder just how pathetic her explanation would sound.

His arm tightened around her waist. "It doesn't matter if you don't want to tell me. I'm only playing with you. You just looked so happy I wanted to know what caused it." He landed a kiss on her lips. "I want to learn what makes you smile, so I can do more of it."

Her heart melted at his explanation, and she had to tell him. She looked up into his eyes. "That's exactly, what made me smile. Don't think I haven't noticed. You do it with so many little things. You pay attention. You know what I like, and you notice when I don't have it."

His hand came up and stroked her cheek. "That's what being in—" He stopped and frowned. "That's …" He shrugged. "It's who I am."

Her heart hammered in her chest as she wondered what he'd been about to say. But he'd chosen not to say it, so she had to let it go. "Exactly, that's who you are, and you're wonderful." She smiled. "And the part I didn't want to say is that you're so different from … from what I was used to." She rested her head against his shoulder. She didn't want to explain what she had been used to. She'd been a fool to put up with it so long. She knew that now, but she hadn't at the time. She'd given her life to her marriage. She'd accepted that over the years, the magic died away. She'd thought that Paul's lack of attention and affection were just how it went after you'd been married for so long.

Manny's arms tightened around her, crushing her against his chest. He kissed the top of her head, and his voice was husky when he spoke. "He didn't deserve you, Nina."

Her head snapped up. She'd always been so careful not to speak badly of Paul. She didn't think that she'd painted him too badly to Manny.

He held her gaze for a long moment. His eyes were gentle, but that pulse was working in his jaw. "I'm sorry. I shouldn't have said that, but I can't help it."

She nodded.

"Don't look so shocked. It's not hard to figure out what you were used to. He didn't pay attention to you. He didn't treasure you. He didn't …"

She put her finger to his lips. It was all true. But she didn't need to hear it, and Manny didn't need to know it. "It doesn't matter anymore."

His hand closed around the back of her neck, and she closed her eyes. She'd said it didn't matter because she wanted him to stop talking. But when he held her like this it was true—nothing mattered anymore except the feel of this wonderful man who was sharing her house, sharing her bed and who, she had to admit, she wanted to share her life.

Manny wanted to tell her that he knew about Paul—knew about the girlfriend. He wasn't one to lie about anything, even by omission. But if he told her, he'd have to tell her how he knew. And that was Ivan's secret, not his. He rested his chin on top of her head and decided he'd have to talk to Ivan. He didn't want there to be any secrets between Nina and him. Then again, she could tell him about it herself if she chose to. He wanted her to be able to open up to him—to want to. It'd come, with time—he hoped.

He stepped away from her with a smile. "Well, I am good at noticing and making sure you get what you want. And it'd be remiss of me not to notice that your fresh coffee is getting cold. He went to the fridge and handed her the cream.

She held his gaze for a long moment when she took it. "I wasn't trying to push you away, you know."

He was back at her side in an instant, his arms around her yet again. "I didn't think you were. I spoke out of turn."

"No. You didn't. You were right, and I'm glad you said it, glad that you see it. I said it doesn't matter because it really doesn't. Whatever my marriage was like is in the past. I know better now." She smiled. "I know that I'm worth more than that."

He couldn't help dropping a kiss on her lips. "You're worth so much more than that. You deserve the best."

She chuckled and tapped her finger in the middle of his chest. "And I believe I found him."

He caught her hand and brought it up to kiss her fingers. "You have, and I want to give you the best—of everything."

The blood surged in his veins as she pressed her hips against his. "Is that an offer to take me back to bed? Show me the best time?"

He loved that she was so eager to make love to him. And he wasn't about to say no. He dropped his head and claimed her mouth in a kiss that should leave her no doubt as to his answer.

She took hold of his hand and started leading him toward the stairs. Instead, he guided her into the living room.

"No?" she asked. "Did you change your mind?"

"Only about going upstairs."

"Oh."

She'd told him a while ago that she wouldn't mind getting more adventurous, and they had—in the bedroom. But so far, they hadn't taken it outside the bedroom. He smiled as he unbuttoned the front of her nightshirt. "We can go up there if you want to."

He loved the way her breasts rose and fell, slightly flushed to match her cheeks. She shook her head. "I don't want to." She put her hand to his shoulder and pushed him back to the sofa.

He sat down and hot waves of desire coursed through him when she pointed at his pants. "You should probably get rid of those."

He pushed them down and kicked out of them before holding his hands up to her. She started to turn, as if to sit in his lap, but he took hold of her hips and brought her down face to face with him, straddling him. Making him ache to be inside her.

"Oh!"

He chuckled and circled her nipple with his thumb. "I want you."

She writhed against him. "I want you, too."

He slid his hand between her legs, touching, teasing, and discovering that she not only wanted him, but was ready for him.

She lifted her hips, and he had to close his eyes when her fingers curled around him, stroking herself with his sensitive head. "I want you now."

He didn't need telling twice. His hands grasped her hips, pulling her down onto him as he thrust hard, burying himself in her wet heat. He let his head fall back against the sofa, luxuriating in the feel of her. He wanted to hold still and draw out the moment, the connection, but she started to move, rocking her hips, lifting up then taking him back deep inside. He let out a low growl. She felt so damned good.

His hands came up of their own volition and closed around her full, plump breasts drawing them closer. Her hands grasped his shoulders when he licked and sucked. The little moan that escaped her lips made him thrust hard.

"Manny!" He loved the way she spoke his name, especially like this, when her voice trembled with need and pleasure.

"Tell me what you want."

"You!" She rocked her hips faster and he moved with her.

He slid his hand between them and caressed the little nub that he knew gave her so much pleasure. It gave him pleasure to see her throw her head back and ride him harder.

He grasped her ass and let her carry him away. She was so close he could feel it, and when she tipped over the edge, she let out another moan that triggered his release. She tightened around him, drawing him deeper, and as waves of pleasure crashed through him, he gave himself to her in every way he knew how.

When they stilled, she collapsed against him, breathing hard. He held her close to his chest, knowing that he didn't ever want to let her go.

She lifted her head and smiled down at him. "You really are the best. You're amazing."

He pulled her head down and kissed her deeply. "*We* are the best. Magic like this only happens between two people who …" He managed to stop himself before he said it. That was twice this morning. He was going to have to find the right moment to tell her how he felt; he didn't want to just let it slip like that. "Who care about each other." He smiled, wanting to lighten the moment that he'd almost spoiled. "And who happen to be talented and compatible."

She chuckled. "Well, you can be talented, and I'll happily be compatible with you."

He eased her off his lap. "You're talented, too."

She made a face. "I'm out of practice."

"That doesn't mean you're not talented. I plan to give you all the practice you can take."

She reached up to touch his cheek and the look in her eyes made him wish he'd chosen this moment to tell her how he felt.

"I'll take whatever you want to give me."

He held her gaze for a long moment and then nodded. He hoped she meant that because he wanted to give her the world.

Chapter Sixteen

Teresa refilled both their glasses and then set the pitcher back down with a smile.

"It's been years since we hung out like this on a Saturday afternoon."

"I know. I don't like to think how many years."

"Then don't. What's gone doesn't matter. All that matters is that we're here right now. It's a beautiful day, not too hot. I have you back—I missed you while you were in Stanton, you know."

Nina smiled. "I missed you, too, but I needed it. I'm glad I'm back, but I think that time away did me good."

"You can say that again. I was worried about you before you left. Since Paul … you … well, you know what you were like; you don't need me to tell you."

Nina nodded and took a sip of her lemonade. "Yeah. That first year was awful. I don't know what I would have done if Abbie hadn't come home. I hated that she felt she had to take care of me, but I don't think I would have made it without her. Not financially. Not emotionally. Not at all."

"Everything worked out for the best in the end. If Abbie hadn't come home, she wouldn't have met Ivan."

Nina took a big gulp of her drink.

"What?" Teresa gave her a puzzled look. "What's wrong?"

Nina gave her a rueful smile. "Am I totally transparent?"

"What makes you ask that?"

"Every time I have a thought and then think I should keep it to myself, someone notices. You just did it. Manny does it all the time."

"That doesn't mean you're transparent. It means that you have people who care about you and who pay attention to what's going on with you."

"Yeah. I guess I'm just not used to that."

Teresa nodded. "I doubt Janet ever noticed what was going on with you."

"No. She didn't. But I wasn't thinking about her."

"Pft. Well, it goes without saying that Paul didn't."

Nina shrugged.

"Anyway, nice distraction tactic, but you still need to tell me what you were thinking. I said everything had worked out for the best and you tried to drown yourself in your lemonade rather than agree with me. Don't you agree? Is Ivan not as wonderful as he seems?"

"No! It's not that. You know I love him to little pieces. He really is the best thing that ever happened to her. I wasn't thinking about Ivan. I wasn't even disagreeing with you. If I'm honest, I agree with you wholeheartedly. It's just … well, it doesn't feel right to say that everything worked out for the best because Paul died. How can anyone dying be the best? It's sad that he didn't get to live the rest of his life. It's worked out better for me because I don't have to live through everything that would have happened—we would have gotten divorced. I have no doubt it would have gotten ugly. But how can him dying be a good thing in any way? How could it ever be the best thing?"

"Yeah. I know what you mean. But he did. You can't change it. You didn't cause it. It is what it is. You can either get lost in grief and guilt that it worked out well for you, or you can let it go. Be grateful that it has worked out this well for you."

Nina nodded and blew out a sigh.

"Oh, stop it!" Teresa pushed at her arm. "I understand where you're coming from, but you can't tell me that you're not grateful to have met Manny?"

She couldn't resist the smile that spread across her face. "No, I can't. I think part of me feeling so guilty is that I feel like he's the best thing that ever happened to me."

Teresa grinned at her. "Now, we're getting down to it. It sure seems that way to me. But I didn't want to say so. Are things getting serious between you guys?"

Nina shrugged. "I think so. But I don't really know."

"What do you mean? Haven't you talked about it?"

She pursed her lips. "We have, but not really."

"Okay, you're going to have to spell it out for me. I don't understand, either you have or you haven't. Is he going to stay? That's the first step, right?"

"I think so."

"But you haven't talked about it?" Teresa was frowning now.

"Kind of. He's gone to see Dan Benson this afternoon. He's talking about doing some freelancing for him. That would say he's staying. And …" She smiled, thinking about all the little things he'd said that indicated that he saw her as part of his future. "And he talks about things he'd like for us to do."

"But you guys haven't talked about what will happen at the end of the month? He hasn't said he's staying, and you haven't asked him to?"

"Nope."

Teresa made a face. "Are you going to?"

"I … I've kind of been waiting for him to say that he wants to. It's all happened so fast, you know?"

"I get it, but …" Teresa sighed. "Oh, what do I know? I'm just feeling protective. I don't want you getting all caught up in it and then him leaving. But … and this will probably sound weird … I trust him. You can just tell that he's totally into you. He's not going to mess you around. I suppose I'm just impatient. I want to hear that you two have it all figured out and are getting on with your happily ever after."

Nina laughed. "I thought happily ever afters were reserved for fairy tale princesses and knights in shining armor—or at least, only for girls half our age."

"No way! You totally deserve one, and there's no reason you shouldn't get one." She grinned. "And besides, if you get to live happily ever after with the delicious Manny, it'll give me hope that I might meet someone someday, too."

"In that case, I'll do my best—for your sake as well as mine."

"Do your best just for you. If I know you, you probably haven't told or shown Manny just how much you care. Maybe you should. I know he's the big strong alpha type, but that doesn't mean you should make him do all the running."

"What do you mean?"

"Well, if he wants to stay here—stay with you, have a future with you, it shouldn't be all on him to say so, should it? Don't make him impose himself in your life. If you want him to be part of your life, why don't you invite him into it?"

"Yeah." Nina nodded to herself as she thought about it. Teresa was right. She'd been going along with things, waiting to see how Manny felt, waiting to hear what he had say, to learn what he wanted. That was how she'd lived her life with Paul. She hadn't thought about it before, but she had just as much power to say what she felt and what she wanted. It was scary to think about putting that out there and being rejected, but that shouldn't be reason to stop her.

She'd already seen where keeping quiet about her feelings got her. If she wanted Manny to see her as an equal, as his partner, then it was only right that she should put herself out there and share the work. If she let him do all the running then she'd only end up following in his shadow, just like she'd always done with Paul.

Teresa smiled at her. "I've got you thinking, haven't I?"

"You have. I know you're right."

"Then let's move on. I don't want to nag you, and I know it's none of my business. I'm only sticking my nose in because I care and I want to see you happy. What's he up to today, anyway? I thought you'd want to make the most of the weekends together since you're working so much in the week."

Nina had to smile. "I am working a lot but we're making the most of the evenings."

Teresa waggled her eyebrows. "Want to tell me more about that?"

"No. I'll leave it to your imagination. Like I said, he's meeting with Dan this afternoon. Dan's building some kind of team."

"Yeah, I heard about that. I thought it was all computer security work. Audrey's son's working for him doing that. But I'm guessing it must be more than that if Manny's going to work with him. He's not a computer guy, is he? And that Ryan Brady. Have you seen him around? You don't need muscles like that to work on computers. I heard a rumor that he's CIA."

"He's an old friend of Manny's, apparently. At least, they've worked together in the past, so I wouldn't be surprised if the rumors are true."

"How do you feel about that?"

Nina frowned. "About what?"

"About Manny doing that kind of work. I mean, I guess it'd be secret stuff, wouldn't it?"

"I suppose so. I don't really know. But … it's who he is; it's what he does."

"Yeah, and it's different from Paul. At least with Manny you'll know he has secrets and why he's keeping them."

Nina stared at her for a long moment. It was true that Paul had kept so much secret from her. But that was different."

~ ~ ~

Manny looked around the building and then back at Dan. "It all sounds good to me. I like the way you've set things up."

"Thanks."

Ryan grinned at him. "I do, too. I like everything about this. We're going to have some fun."

Dan laughed. "I'm not sure it's going to be enough fun for you. This will be a lot less exciting than what you're used to."

"Nah. I'm not as old and past it as Manny here, but I'm ready to slow things down. I've spent my whole career in the field. I think this is going to be the perfect compromise." He winked at Manny. "It'll be slowing things down for me, but stepping things up for you. Are you sure you're up to it, old man?"

Manny jabbed his arm. "You can quit with the old man crap."

Dan laughed. "I can already see it's going to be a handful having you both on board."

Ryan slung his arm around Manny's shoulders. "Nah. We'll be good. We're only playing. If I really thought Manny was past it, I wouldn't be joking about it and I wouldn't want to work with him. And if he thought I was as full of shit as I pretend to be, he'd pass, too, right?"

Manny nodded. "Yep. You have nothing to worry about, Dan. We're good. For all the shit we give each other, I'd rather this guy had my back than just about anyone else I know."

"And I'd rather this old fart had my back than anyone else."

Manny slapped the back of his head. "I've told you to quit with the old man crap."

Dan shook his head with a smile. "I don't know about retiring from your respective agencies; it seems to me you're more like a pair of kids."

"Rejuvenated, that's what we are," said Ryan.

"I like it," said Manny. That was exactly how he felt. In his last few weeks at work, he'd been feeling old, feeling as though the future was just a long slow road to nowhere, that his retirement would be a period that he needed to fill with whatever he could find. Now, just a few weeks in, he'd landed himself a job, which even though it wouldn't be full-time, filled him with more enthusiasm than anything he'd worked on in years. And even better, he'd met Nina. Sure, he was excited about working with Dan and Ryan, but he was more excited about the future that he and Nina might build.

Dan checked his watch. "Well, if you've heard all you need to, I'd better get going. I said I'd meet Missy at the Boathouse when we were done here."

They all made their way out into the parking lot of the building that Dan had bought and renovated to be the headquarters of his new operation. Manny and Ryan watched him pull away.

"What do you think?" asked Ryan. "Do you want to come get a beer with me? Shoot the shit and trade old war stories?"

Manny laughed. "I'd love to. But I won't stay long. Just the one."

Ryan raised an eyebrow. "You have other plans?"

"Yeah."

Ryan chuckled. "I know you do. Want to tell me all about her?"

"No."

"Aww. And I thought we were buddies."

"We are, and it's because we're buddies that I already know your cynical take on women, and I don't want to hear you apply it to Nina."

Ryan rolled his eyes. "I'm only cynical about the women I meet. I'm cursed. I accept the possibility that they're not all bad. I'm even kind of hopeful that you might have met a good one. That's why I want to hear about her."

"Seriously?"

Ryan grinned. "Seriously. You're going to need someone to take care of you in your old age."

Manny had to laugh. "Okay. I'll see you at the Boathouse. But like I said, I'm not staying for long."

"She got you whipped already?"

"Nope. It's not that I *have* to get back to her, it's that I *want* to."

Manny's phone rang when he pulled up in the square outside the Boathouse. He glanced over at where Ryan was just getting out of his car and then glanced at the display. He pursed his lips when he saw Kim's name. He'd said he'd call to check in with her and Andrés once he got settled here at the lake and he hadn't made the time to yet.

"Come on," called Ryan as he got out of the car.

Manny held his phone up. "I need to take this. I'll be right with you. You can get me a beer."

Ryan nodded and made his way to the restaurant.

"Hi, Kim."

"Hey. How's it going? We were just talking about you this morning—wondering how you're liking Summer Lake. I guessed that you're not loving it and you don't want to tell us that. Andrés said you're probably too busy having a good time and that's why you forgot to call."

Manny laughed. "Well, I'm sure he'll love it when you tell him that he was right."

"He is? You are? You're loving it? Oh, Manny, that's wonderful. Tell me all about it?"

"I will, but not now. I'm just about to meet up with an old friend but I didn't want to ignore your call."

"Oh. Anyone we know?"

"No. Just a guy I used to work with."

"Okay, well I won't keep you—as long as you promise you'll check in soon. I want to hear all about it. Do you think you're going to stay there?"

"Yeah. I am." Manny started walking across the parking lot. "When's a good time?"

"Tomorrow afternoon? We're out this evening, but we're having a quiet day tomorrow."

"Okay. I'll call you then."

"I'll look forward to it. Before I let you go, though, you have to tell me one thing."

He laughed. "One thing? Just anything?"

Kim laughed with him. "No. Not just anything. One thing in particular. Tell me the reason you're having such a good time there … is it a woman?"

"Yeah. It is."

"Oh, Manny! That's so wonderful I've had this feeling that you were going to meet someone. I want to hear all about her. I want to meet her."

He pushed open the door to the restaurant and spotted Ryan who was waving to him from the bar. "You will. I'll tell you both about her tomorrow and then at some point we'll figure out when we can meet up. I have to go now, though, Kim."

"Okay. I won't keep you. But you know if you don't call, I'll be calling you."

He laughed. "Yeah, I do. Talk to you tomorrow."

"Yep, and Manny?"

"Yeah?"

"Say hello to her for me? Tell her I can't wait to meet her. Unless … she won't think it's weird, will she?"

"No. She knows about you, knows that we're all still close." He smiled when he remembered Nina's reaction. "She thought it was nice."

"Aww. That's good. It worries me you know. Some women can be weird about exes. I'd hate to think that our still being friends might ever make things difficult for you when you're dating someone."

Manny nodded. He wasn't just dating Nina. It was so much more than that. But if he told Kim that he'd never get her off the phone. "Don't worry. It's not a problem."

"Okay. I'll let you go."

"Bye." He ended the call and took a seat at the bar next to Ryan who handed him a beer.

"There you go. If you're not staying long, you'd better start talking."

Manny laughed. "If that's your interrogation technique, I can see why they kicked you out."

Ryan rolled his eyes. "They didn't. It was my choice to get out."

"Want to tell me why?"

Ryan took a slug of his beer and nodded slowly. "Probably. If I get around to talking about it to anyone, you'll be my first choice. But not now. Let's just say I'm ready to live what's left of my life for me. And this seems like a good place to do it. For now, I'm more interested in you. What made you choose Summer Lake? And what's so special about this woman that you've decided to stay?"

"The first question's easy. I came up here a while back on a job. Morales—remember him?"

"Damn, yeah, I do. And I heard what happened with Zack Águila, Diego's son. It didn't click. I heard that Diego's here now."

"That's right. Zack moved up here a couple of years ago. Diego came more recently. I came to take care of Morales when he tracked Zack here. It's a good little town. When I was starting to think about where I wanted to go when I retired it seemed like a good option. Then when I found out that Diego and Ted had moved here, too …" He shrugged. "I thought I'd give it a try."

"And now you've tried it and you like it. That's the easy part—for you to explain and for me to understand. What about the woman?"

Manny frowned. "Nina. Her name's Nina."

Ryan laughed and grasped his shoulder. "And your reaction there should tell me all I need to know. She's not just a woman, right? She has a name and you need me to know it."

Manny smiled through pursed lips. "Yeah. That's about it. I wish I could tell you why I feel the way I do. I'm not, I've never …" He shook his head. "I wasn't factoring a woman into my retirement plans, but …"

Ryan squeezed his shoulder. "Hey, I know I can be an asshole about women, but if she makes you happy, then I'm happy for you."

"Thanks. I take it your views on women haven't changed?"

Ryan made a face. "Nah. Like I said, I think I'm cursed."

Kenzie the bartender came over and winked at Manny. "He keeps saying that he's cursed when it comes to women, but I've told him, there's no curse strong enough to stand up to the magic of Summer Lake."

Manny smiled. Kenzie loved to play matchmaker, but he didn't think even she would get anywhere with trying to pair Ryan off. "I don't know, Kenzie. I wouldn't hold your breath with this one."

Kenzie laughed. "We'll just have to wait and see, won't we?"

Ryan laughed with her and said something, but Manny was no longer paying attention. He'd spotted at guy at the other end of the bar who looked a lot like the guy in the mugshot Colt had sent him of Brian.

Ryan picked up on the change in him. "What is it?"

Manny turned to him with a frown. "Nina's had a problem with a guy stalking her. He's …" He looked back to the end of the bar, but the guy had gone.

Ryan followed his gaze. "What do you need?"

It felt good to know he had someone like Ryan as backup, but right now all that mattered to him was getting back to Nina. "I need to go and make sure she's okay."

Ryan nodded. "Text me everything you have on him when you get a minute, but before you go, do you have a photo?"

Manny pulled out his phone and sent the picture.

"I'll keep an eye out. Let me know what you need."

"Thanks." Manny got to his feet. "I'll give you a call."

His heart thundered in his chest as he jogged across the square back to his car. He'd been following Nina to work, dropping in on her throughout the day. Other than work they were mostly together. Had he let his guard down too far today? He hit the button on the steering wheel to call her as he pulled out. He'd be back at the house in a couple of minutes, but he couldn't wait that long to know she was all right.

"Hi."

His heart rate steadied at the sound of her voice. "Hey. I'm on the way back."

"Oh, good. I just got in."

"I'll see you in a couple of minutes."

"Manny, what's wrong?"

"Nothing."

"Yes, there is. I can hear it in your voice."

"It's okay. There's nothing to worry about. I'll tell you in a minute. I'm almost there."

Chapter Seventeen

"Are you awake?"

"Hmm?"

"Never mind. Go back to sleep."

Nina smiled and snuggled closer against him. She was almost ready to wake up, but this felt so good. She was warm and cozy, Manny's arm was tight around her middle. His hard chest pressed against her back, and judging by the way he was getting harder against her ass, he was ready to wake up.

Shivers chased each other down her back when he kissed the back of her neck.

"Mmm." It felt so good. She knew what was coming next. They'd started enough mornings this way that she knew that as he kissed her neck, he pulled her back closer against him, his arm held her tight while his fingers traveled up and down her stomach. She relaxed against him, looking forward to—

"I'll get the coffee started."

She felt him move away, heard his feet hit the floor and by the time she'd rolled over, he was pulling on a pair of sweatpants.

"I wasn't thinking about coffee." She held her hand out to him, hoping that he'd change his mind and come back into bed, finish what she'd hoped he was starting.

He gave her a rueful smile. "I need to get up."

"Okay." She sat up and pulled the sheet over her as she watched him leave the room. His broad shoulders taunted her as he went, her fingers itched to touch him. But he disappeared without looking back.

It left her feeling cold and more alone than she'd ever felt when she'd lived in this house by herself. She didn't think there was anything wrong with him … between them. She knew it was ridiculous to feel this way about him getting up abruptly. She'd done it herself many mornings.

She hugged the sheet tighter to her chest and blew out a sigh. Her reaction wasn't about the way he'd gotten up. No, it was about the realization that he could get up and walk out of her life just as easily. She didn't think he wanted to. He'd told her in dozens of different ways that he wanted to be with her—that she was his, even. But she'd never come out and told him how important he'd become to her. She hadn't told him that she wanted him in her life. Sure, she'd agreed with him when he said things like that, but still …

She got up and pulled on the shorts and tank top that served as her summer pajamas. Teresa had been right yesterday. She shouldn't make him do all the running. She should let him know that she wanted him to stay—here, in the house, in her life. His month was almost over, and they hadn't talked about what would happen when it was.

He greeted her with a kiss when she reached the kitchen and jerked his chin toward the coffee pot. "It won't be a minute. Sorry about that. I … I can't stop thinking about Brian."

She frowned. "You don't even know if it was him that you saw last night."

He pursed his lips. "I don't know for sure, but if it wasn't him, then it was my subconscious mind giving me a nudge. I'd let my guard down."

She laughed. "Let your guard down? You go with me to work every morning. You check in on me a couple times a day. The few times I go anywhere without you, I'd swear I feel you watching over me." She made a face at him. "I haven't asked you, but you do, don't you? You keep an eye on me."

He shrugged. "It's what I do. But I wasn't keeping an eye on you yesterday. You were at Teresa's, and I was at Dan's office and then at the Boathouse with Ryan."

"For just a few hours."

"I know, but if he's going to make a move, it'll only take a few minutes, not hours."

A shiver ran down her spine as she remembered the smile on Brian's face when he'd grabbed her in the alley.

Manny came to her and closed his arms around her. "Sorry. This is why I got up. I knew you'd need coffee before we started talking about him."

She chuckled against his chest. "I need coffee no matter what."

He stepped away from her and poured them each a mug. Nina took hers and sat at the counter to add cream and sugar.

"Aren't you scared?"

She shrugged. She didn't know how he'd feel if she answered that truthfully.

"Would you mind if I run him off?"

She met his gaze. "What exactly does that mean?"

Manny shrugged and took a sip of his coffee instead of answering.

Nina wasn't sure she wanted him to explain. "To answer your first question, I'm really not scared. I don't know if this is good or bad … but with you around, I don't see how I could be scared. Then again, feeling that way scares me in a different way. I don't want you to just see me as someone you have to rescue."

He slung his arm around her shoulders and pulled her into his side. "I don't. You're not someone I need to rescue. You're … mine. I meant it when I said that. You're mine and protecting you is … well, it's like I'm protecting a piece of me." He dropped a kiss on her lips. "It's about protecting my heart."

"Aww. You keep surprising me with the beautiful things you say." Her heart was hammering. She had to let him know that she felt the same way. It was her turn to step up and do more than just thank him or agree with him when he expressed the way he felt about her.

"I don't think you know how much that means to me." She reached up and touched his cheek. "How much you've come to mean to me. I trust you to do whatever you think is best. Run him off, draw him out, whatever. I trust you and I know you'll keep me safe."

"I promise."

"I can't wait until he's dealt with. Until he's no longer a threat or a shadow hanging over me. I feel like he's the last negative hangover from my life before we met." She met his gaze. "And I'm so ready to get started on my new life—my life with you."

His eyes widened, and she had to hope she hadn't said too much.

His smile reassured her, and the way he kissed her confirmed everything that she'd hoped. He wanted her in his life, and he was thrilled that she'd told him.

When he lifted his head, his eyes were shining happily. "You want it? You want me?"

She nodded. "More than anything."

He closed his arms around her and held her close to his chest. "I've been biding my time, not wanting to go too fast, not wanting to rush you … not wanting to blow this. The month's almost over and I didn't know what … didn't know when I should—"

She put a finger up to his lips. It felt good to be the one giving reassurance instead of seeking it. "I know. And it's not fair that you should be the one to have to figure it all out. That's why I told you. I know what I want; it was time for me to say so. And now we can figure it out together."

She had to laugh as he lifted her off the stool and twirled her around. "Do you want to take a drive over to the other side of the lake?" he asked as he sat her back down.

She cocked her head to one side, not understanding.

He chuckled. "Sorry. I mean, do you want to go look at the houses over there? Now, that I know you want me, we need to find ourselves a place."

Her throat went dry, and she looked around the kitchen. "This is a place." She'd thought he liked it here.

Manny's smile faded. "I know, but … I thought … We … I …"

Nina jumped when her phone rang. She wanted to ignore it but she couldn't. It was terrible timing, but then again, perhaps it wasn't. Manny obviously needed a minute to figure out what he wanted to say. And she needed one to figure out how she felt. "I'd better get that."

Manny nodded and watched her pick up her phone and take it through to the living room. "Morning, Abbie. No. it's okay."

He blew out a sigh and ran a hand through his hair. Shit! He'd blown that. He'd been so thrilled that she was inviting him into her life. He'd been waiting and wanting to ask if she wanted him to stick around. But he'd gotten carried away. When he realized that she was on the same page as him, he'd moved on to the next one—the one where they'd find the house they were going to live in. He should have waited; he should have been patient. Should have enjoyed the moment before trying to hurry along to the next one. He knew the steps he wanted them to take, but Nina didn't.

He looked around the kitchen. He had to hope that her reaction had only been shock at his timing—not an indication that she didn't want to leave this place. If she didn't, he'd deal with it. But he wanted them to find their own house. He wanted them to make a home of their own to live their life together in. He scowled. He would if he had to, but he didn't like the idea of living here in the house she'd shared with Paul. Of course, he wanted a nicer place, but more than that, he wanted a place that would be their own—the place where they built their future and moved away from her past.

He took a big gulp of coffee. It'd be all right. He just needed to dial it back a bit. Take things at her pace. He didn't mind how long it took for her to be ready to move in with him.

What mattered was that she'd come out and told him that she wanted him in her life. There was nothing in their way.

He scowled. Well, that wasn't entirely true. He needed to find this Brian and run him off once and for all. He didn't need to wait around and be on the defensive. He glanced at the clock on the wall. It was still early. He might even be able to take care of it today.

Nina had talked about maybe seeing Abbie today. If she did, he could use that time to find Brian.

His phone buzzed with a text, and he picked it up half expecting it to be Kim reminding him that he needed to call them today.

It wasn't, it was Ryan.

Found him.

He's camping down by the lake.

Want me to take care of it?

No. Manny needed to take care of this one himself. He dialed Ryan's number and waited.

"I can take care of it if you want. He won't ever bother you or your lady again." Ryan answered without a hello.

Manny smiled through pursed lips. "It's tempting. But no."

"I had a feeling you'd say that. You need to do it yourself, right?"

"Yeah. That and I know you'd never tell me what you'd done—I'd forever wonder."

Ryan laughed. "You shouldn't believe everything you hear about me. I'm not that bad."

"Perhaps not. But the curiosity would kill me, and I know you'd never tell."

"You got that right. Do you want me to meet you and show you where he is?"

Manny glanced through the door to where Nina was chatting happily in the living room with her daughter. "Yeah. How long do you need?"

"No time like the present."

"Okay. Where?"

"Meet me in the parking lot by the public beach."

"I'll be there in ten."

He hung up and watched Nina do the same. She came back into the kitchen with a wary smile on her face.

"Is everything okay?"

She nodded. "Yes. Abbie and Ivan want to know if we'd like to go over for dinner." She made a face. "I said I'd ask. It doesn't matter if you don't want—"

He put a finger to her lips, just as she'd done to him earlier. "I do want to. I'd love to." He planted a kiss on her forehead. "And I'd also like to talk about what just happened here— what I said about looking at houses. But there's something I need to do first. That was Ryan on the phone."

Her eyes widened. "He kind of scares me."

Manny chuckled. "He's a good guy. He's going to—"

She shook her head. "I don't think I want to know."

Manny frowned, but she shook her head again.

"You're going to be working with him. From what you've said, most of what you're doing will be secret, right?"

He nodded.

"So, why not start as we mean to go on? You go do whatever it is you need to do. I'm going to sit in the sun for a while."

"Okay. I don't expect I'll be very long."

She smiled. "You do what you need to. I'll be here."

He closed his arms around her and hugged her to his chest. He didn't know if she'd guessed that this was about Brian, but he was glad he didn't have to explain. "Do you want me to pick us up some breakfast on the way back?"

"No, just let me know when you're on the way. I'll make something."

"You take such good care of me, but you don't have to, you know."

She smiled. "I want to; I like it. It's who I am. Just like you take care of me in the ways that come naturally to you."

He dropped a kiss on the top of her head. Her explanation helped him. He didn't like to think that she was putting herself out to do for him, but it didn't feel like he was putting himself out to take care of her. He was just being who he was. If she were doing the same, then he'd relax about it.

Ryan was waiting for him when he pulled up in the parking lot.

"I did some asking around last night after you left. But he wasn't staying at the resort and I couldn't find anything else on him. Then I got lucky this morning. I was going into the convenience store as he was coming out. I followed him. He's camping just on the other side of those trees." He pointed at a stand of trees on the far side of the parking lot. "You want me to come with you?"

"No. Thanks. This one's personal."

"Oh, I know."

Manny made a face. "Maybe stay within earshot? I'm only going to warn him off. I expect words will be all it takes, but it wouldn't do any harm for him to see that I have back up."

"Absolutely." Ryan grinned. "Even when you're done, I'll mess with his head till he leaves."

Manny frowned.

Ryan held his hands up. "I won't touch him, won't even go near him, but I'll let him know how it feels to be stalked, how about that?"

Manny chuckled. "That sounds perfect, Thanks, Ryan."

Ryan grasped his shoulder. "I'm glad to be able to help out. Honestly. I know I give you shit, but I owe you big time. I've never forgotten that. I never will."

Manny waved a hand. "You should. I have."

"Never. But quit standing around here listening to me go soft. Get your ass in there and run this asshole out of town."

Manny made his way through the trees without making a sound. He watched the tent for a few moments wondering if he'd need to approach. He didn't need to wonder long. The zipper went up and Brian came out. He didn't have the look of a crazy. But Manny knew that the way people looked and the way they acted didn't always match up.

He stepped forward when Brian turned back to close the tent. He spun around and made Manny's lip curl with contempt when he cowered and held his hands up as if to defend himself.

"Stop! I don't … oh … it's you."

Manny had wondered whether he'd been watching Nina, whether he'd seen Manny with her. It seemed he had. He nodded grimly. "Yeah. It's me."

"What do you want? What are you doing here?"

Manny wanted nothing more than to take him by the throat and … No. He had to get a grip. "You got the questions right, but you need to answer them, not ask them."

Brian dropped his gaze.

"What do you think you're doing here?" Manny's voice sounded low and threatening even to his own ears.

"Nina."

Manny's hands balled into fists at his sides. "Nina told you she didn't want to see you again."

"But … she didn't give me a chance. I love her. I want her to get to know me and then she'll love me back …" He met Manny's gaze and scowled. "But then she left and now you're in the way."

Manny shook his head. "She left because you attacked her."

The way he smiled made Manny's blood run cold. "I was trying to love her."

He might not look crazy, but he was sure as hell sounding it. "She doesn't want you to love her. She's never going to love you. You need to leave her alone." He'd come here ready to do whatever it took to make sure that Brian never bothered Nina again. He'd have been happy to get his message across with his fists. The last thing he'd expected was to end up trying to explain things to someone who sounded and acted like a small child.

Brian nodded sadly. "I saw. She loves you. You love her."

Manny's heart pounded in his chest. It was true, but he'd be damned if Brian was going to be the first person he admitted that to.

"But *I* want to love her."

Manny hated the way he said that. It forewarned another attack as far as he was concerned. He spun around when he heard a twig crack. Ryan emerged from the trees and gave him a meaningful look before he smiled at Brian.

"Hey, Brian. I've been looking for you."

"Who are you?"

"I'm Ryan. I've come to take you back."

Brian scowled. "I don't want to go back. They said I could go home."

"Yeah, but you were supposed to keep taking your medication, weren't you?"

Manny was fascinated at the way he dropped his head, looking for all the world like a guilty kid who'd been called out for not doing his homework.

"I lost them."

"Yeah, well. Your mom's been worried about you. She wants you to come back to the hospital and then come home with her."

His eyes lit up. "I can stay with Mom?"

"Yeah, that's right, buddy. Do you want me to give you a ride back to the hospital?"

"Okay."

Manny caught Ryan's gaze with a *what the fuck?* look.

"Do you want to take your tent down?" asked Ryan.

Brian nodded and obediently set to work.

Manny pulled Ryan aside. "What's going on?"

"I called the plates in to Don after I texted you this morning. He just got back to me. Apparently, Brian here has dissociative identity disorder."

Manny raised an eyebrow.

"They used to call it multiple personality disorder."

"Ah." Manny glanced at Brian who was busily taking his tent down, again reminding him of an obedient child.

"Yeah. I don't know how it slipped through when they booked him. But when Don ran the plates it turns out that the vehicle belongs to his brother. He reported it stolen late last week—along with his camping gear. Apparently, Brian's been doing well for about a year. He's supposed to take antidepressants and antipsychotics. But it seems he's not."

Manny nodded and watched Brian again. He looked up and smiled as he started to fold the tent.

"Damn!"

"Yeah. I know you told me to stand down, but I had to let you know. I understand you probably want to beat him to a pulp but he's—this version of him, at least—is just a little kid."

"How many …?" Manny didn't even know what to think, let alone how to phrase his question. "How many of him are there?"

"I don't know. I got the bare minimum and came in after you."

"Thanks. I owe you one."

Ryan shook his head. "Nah. Why don't you get back to Nina and let her know she's got nothing to worry about anymore?"

"No way. What are you planning to do with him?"

Ryan laughed. "Jesus. Don't look so worried. Don called in the mental health folks and they're going to meet us at the station."

"I should at least come there with you." He couldn't help looking at Brian again. "He could still be dangerous. You don't want to be alone in the vehicle with him."

Ryan shrugged. "We can all ride over there together if you like."

"Yeah. I need to do that. I want to talk to Don. Talk to whoever comes to pick him up." Manny wasn't sure what exactly he needed, but he needed something. Leaving Ryan to handle the situation wasn't going to fly with him.

Chapter Eighteen

Nina set her fork down and shook her head. Manny had told her about Brian while they ate, but she still found it hard to believe.

"Are you okay?"

"Yeah. I'm fine, but it's so strange, you know? I had dinner with him. He was nice enough. He said he worked at the ski resort. He …" She shook her head. "He said he enjoyed fishing, he talked about his family—his mom and his brother. He didn't do or say anything that would indicate that he was … that he had … What's it called again?"

"Dissociative identity disorder." Manny blew out a sigh. "I'd never heard of it. Multiple personality disorder. Honestly, before today I would have called it schizophrenia, but apparently that's a common misconception. The mental health services guys who came to pick him up explained it a bit. I wanted to know how he could have seemed so normal to you and yet the Brian I talked to this morning was like a little kid. They said that it's like being completely different people, different personalities—they're called alters. One of Brian's alters is the little kid. One of them, the one you knew, I guess, is the regular Brian. He has others, too."

"I don't know what to think. I don't know how to feel even. I feel bad, like I should have known, should have been able to help him somehow."

Manny took hold of her hand. "No. There's no way you could have known and nothing you could do to help. It sounds like his family has been trying to help him for years, but there's only so much they can do. He wants to live with his mom, but she can't handle him. She's said she'll take him in again once they get his medication figured out again."

"And he'll be in the hospital until they do?"

"Yeah. It's not really a hospital; it's a group home."

Nina nodded as if she understood, but she still didn't, not really.

Manny squeezed her hand. "All you need to know is that it's over. You said he was the last shadow hanging over you. Now it's been taken care of." He smiled. "The sun can shine again."

She smiled back at him. "You say such lovely things. You're like a ray of sunshine."

He laughed. "I've been called many things, but never a ray of sunshine."

"Well, you have now. Like you said, the sun's shining so what do you want to do?" If he wanted to go and look at the houses over at Four Mile Creek, she wouldn't mind going. She'd been curious to see them. It didn't mean they had to make any decisions yet.

He glanced at the clock on the wall. "I should probably call Andrés and Kim before we do anything else, get that out of the way."

"Okay."

"And then what do you think about seeing if we can rent a boat at the resort for the afternoon? I haven't been out on the water yet."

"Ooh! I'd love to. I haven't done that in years. Do you like boating?"

"I haven't done any in years. I used to go up to a friend's cabin whenever I had some time off. He had a boat and I used to spend my days on the lake fishing. Do you fish?"

She nodded happily. "I haven't done that in years either. But I used to love it."

"Great. I'll give them a call first to see if they have anything available."

"You call Kim and Andrés. I can take care of it. What time do you want to go?"

"Any time they say. I won't be long, but I do need to check in with them."

Nina smiled. "Tell Kim I said hello back to her."

Manny held her gaze for a moment. "She said she hoped you wouldn't think it was weird that we're still close. Do you?"

"No." She answered automatically. "Well, if I'm honest, I kind of do. Maybe unusual is a better word. I'm more used to hearing people complain about their exes. But I think it's nice. I think it says a lot about who you are as people that you're still friends."

She could tell that he liked her answer. She got up and dropped a kiss on his lips. "I'll go and call the Boathouse."

Manny smiled to himself as he watched the gate swing open when they arrived at Ivan and Abbie's place. It reminded him of Zack and Maria's house. If he was honest, it reminded him of the kind of house he'd like for himself. He glanced over at Nina. He'd deliberately dropped the matter of them going over to Four Mile this afternoon. She'd had enough to deal with learning about Brian. He hadn't wanted to put more pressure on her. Not today. There was no hurry.

She smiled at him. "Are you sure you're okay with this?"

"I'm looking forward to it." He reached for her hand and squeezed it. "Now that I know you want me in your life, I want to become a part of it. She's your daughter. I want to get to know her. I want her to get to know me."

"And Ivan, too."

"Yeah." Manny frowned as he pulled forward and started up the long driveway. She still didn't know that he knew what had really happened with Paul. She didn't know that Ivan knew either.

"Though you do know him a little now." She smiled. "I'm glad you met each other out running. It seems less forced that way. And you know each other on your terms."

He nodded. They did, though he wasn't sure what she'd think if she knew about the conversation they'd had. He didn't like keeping secrets from her. His heart sank. That wasn't the only secret on his mind tonight either. "Am I right in thinking that you still haven't told Abbie about Brian?"

She looked guilty as she shook her head. "I kept waiting for the right moment and it never came. The longer I left it the more difficult it felt. Part of me wants to just let it go now that he's taken care of, but part of me thinks I should tell her—at least, she won't have to worry."

Manny didn't want to tell her what to do, but he hoped that she would.

She raised an eyebrow at him. "You'd tell her if you were in my shoes, wouldn't you?"

He chuckled. "I didn't say a word."

She laughed with him. "No, but you thought it very loudly." Her smile faded. "There are lots of things I haven't told her. But it's to protect her. I didn't want her to worry about me because of Brian. I didn't want to taint her memories of who she thought her dad was." She looked at Manny as he brought the car to a stop. "What would you do?"

He shook his head. "I don't know. I can't tell you what to do, and I have to be honest, I don't know what I'd do myself." He looked up as the front door opened and Abbie came out to greet them.

"Well, I'm definitely not going to say anything to her tonight. Not about her dad, and probably not about Brian either. Are you okay with that?"

"Of course." He'd go along with whatever she wanted.

Abbie reached the car with Ivan close behind her and she pulled Nina's door open. "Hey! Come on in. This is so great." She hugged Nina and then came around to greet Manny when he got out. She gave him a quick hug, too. "Thanks for coming."

"Thanks for inviting me."

Ivan laughed by her side. "She's been wanting to invite you for weeks. But I kept telling her not to be impatient."

Manny was thrilled when Nina came and slid her arm around his waist. "Well, you can invite us over any time you like now." She smiled up at him. "And we'll have to invite you guys over soon, too."

Manny smiled at Ivan. "I grill a mean steak if I can tempt you with that."

Abbie came to link her arm though his and lead them inside. "You can tempt us both with that. But you guys might need to add some variety to your menus. "Ivan's grilling steaks for us tonight."

Manny laughed. "Great minds, huh?"

"Either that or limited chefs," said Nina.

"Hey!" He gave her a mock hurt look. "I do my best when you let me."

"You do wonderfully. But we all know that the cooking is my thing. Your talents are more about keeping people safe than keeping them fed."

Ivan shot him a curious look. He was no doubt wondering about Brian. Manny nodded. "Well, maybe I can get some tips from Ivan on how to feed you better steak. You want to show me to the grill?"

Ivan nodded and led him out back while the girls went to the kitchen to get drinks.

~ ~ ~

Abbie glanced out onto the deck where Manny and Ivan were already laughing about something while Ivan got the steaks ready, then she turned back to Nina. "I'm glad those two have hit it off. I like this, Mom. I like it a lot. How about you? Is it weird for you?"

Nina held her daughter's gaze for a long moment. She knew Abbie was concerned how she might feel about being here with Manny. But she didn't know the truth about Paul. On the one hand, she wanted to reassure her that she was happier than she'd ever been, but how could she do that without explaining how things had really been with Paul?

Abbie started to look worried. "Is it too weird?"

"No. It's really not. I have to be honest with you, Abbs." She wasn't going to be completely honest, she didn't see that anything good would ever come from destroying her memory of her father. She didn't have to tell her the whole truth, but she could be honest about how she felt about Manny. "It feels wonderful. He's a good man. He's good to me, and I …" She stopped herself short. She couldn't say what she'd been about to. She hadn't fully admitted that to herself yet, and when she did, she wanted Manny to be the first person to know. "I care about him very much."

To her relief, Abbie let out a happy little squeal and came to wrap her up in a hug. "That's awesome, Mom. I'm so happy for you. I didn't know if you'd ever be happy again. I'll be honest. I didn't think you'd ever want to be with someone else. And … I know it doesn't matter, but then again, to you, it probably does … what I'm trying to say is that I don't mind. God, that sounds wrong. I just need you to know that I don't have a problem with it. I like him, too. He's great. And it's obvious how he feels about you. I still miss Dad. I always will. And I know you do, too. But he'd want you to be happy, so don't let that stand in the way of wherever you and Manny are going."

Nina's eyes filled with tears. They were tears of gratitude for her wonderful daughter and her big heart, but she knew that Abbie would assume that they were tears for Paul. She felt guilty about it. Part of her still didn't want to let Abbie believe a lie, but the truth would only hurt her.

Abbie hugged her again. "I'm sorry. I didn't mean to upset you."

"You didn't. I'm just grateful that you're so good to me. I love you, Abbs."

"I love you too, Mom."

Nina straightened up and blew her nose. "Anyway."

Abbie smiled. "That's right. We've said our bit. Now we can get on with it. This is about here and now." She smiled. "And I think it's going to be about the future, too. You and Manny, there's a future in it, right?"

Nina nodded.

"Good. Then let's take these drinks out to them and talk and laugh and have fun. Let's get this new beginning off to a great start."

"That sounds good to me." Nina held the door for her as they made their way outside. She hung back and watched as Abbie handed the guys beers and started talking and laughing with them. Looking back, she couldn't remember ever having times like this with Paul. Manny caught her eye and raised an eyebrow. It made her heart happy to know that wonderful man cared about her so much. She hoped he felt the same way she did. She planned to tell him soon the words she hadn't been able to make herself say to Abbie. She loved him, and she already knew in her heart that he loved her, too.

She smiled and went to join them at the grill. Abbie was right, this was about here and now. The right time would come for her to tell Manny that she loved him. Tonight was about relaxing and having fun, the four of them together. Tears pricked her eyes again when she realized that this was her new family.

Manny put his arm around her shoulders and pulled her into his side. He didn't say anything, but his eyes asked if she was all right. She could only hope that her smile could tell him just how happy she was.

It was late when they got back to the house. Manny stood back and watched as Nina unlocked the front door. It didn't feel right to him. He wanted them to be coming home—to their house. He'd be patient if he had to, but he hoped he wouldn't have to be for long.

"Do you want a drink?" she asked.

He leaned in the kitchen doorway and folded his arms across his chest as he watched her pour herself a glass of water.

"I need to dilute some of that wine; otherwise, I'll have a headache in the morning."

He checked his watch. She wasn't going to get a full night's sleep; she had to be at work at seven. "I'm fine. All I want is to take you to bed."

She waggled her eyebrows at him. "And take advantage of me while I'm tipsy?"

He chuckled. "No. And hold you while you sleep. You have work in a few hours."

She shrugged. "I'm used to it."

He wished she didn't have to go. He'd love to think that she might at least cut back to part-time hours soon. He didn't imagine that the gift store would be so busy once the tourist season died down. And she was only supposed to be covering. He didn't say anything. It was too late to get into that conversation and they needed to finish their conversation about where they were going to live first anyway.

She came to him and slipped her arms around his waist. "I'm not too tired."

He took her hand and led her upstairs. "You would be in the morning."

Once they were in bed, she pressed herself against him, and it wasn't easy to deny her, but he knew she'd be asleep in minutes if he let her.

"Did you have a great time tonight?"

"I did. I like Abbie and Ivan. Even if she wasn't your daughter, I'd like them a lot just as people."

She smiled. "That makes me happy."

It made Manny happy, too. "I hope you'll like Andrés and Kim when you meet them next weekend." When he'd talked to them earlier, Kim had insisted that they wanted to come up and visit—and meet Nina.

"I'm sure I will. I'm looking forward to it." She looked up into his eyes. "It felt like you became part of my family tonight."

"It felt that way to me, too. I know Andres and Kim aren't my family, but that's how I feel about you meeting them. I'll take you to see my sisters one of these days as well."

"I'd like that."

He held her close to his chest and loved the way her breathing synced with his. There was so much he wanted to talk about, but none of it was as important as this—just being with her, holding her, loving her.

Brian had said it this morning and it was true. He did love her. He wanted to tell her right now, to whisper it into her hair as she fell asleep. He looked down at her wondering if he should. If this was the right moment.

He had to smile when he saw that her eyes were already closed.

Chapter Nineteen

Nina waved when she saw Teresa sitting waiting for her. She made her way across the deck of the restaurant to join her.

"Hey. Wasn't this a good idea, if I do say so myself?"

"It was. I needed a break today, too. It's been crazy in the gift shop."

Teresa frowned. "How much longer are you going to be there for?"

"I don't know, Ben left a message that he wants to talk to me. I heard that Rebecca might not be coming back. So, I'm keeping my fingers crossed that he might want me to stay on."

"You want to? I thought you'd be looking forward to finishing up in there."

"No! I need the money. You know that."

"I know but … you've got Manny now."

"Pft! I'll pay my own way, thank you."

"I know. I didn't mean it like that, but surely … oh, what do I know. Ignore me. What else is going on with you?"

"Other than work and Manny, not much. Tell me about you? It seems like we only ever talk about me these days."

"Because you have so much excitement going on. I don't have anything good to talk about."

"Does that mean you have something not so good?"

Teresa made a face. "Yeah, but you have to promise me that if I tell you about it, you have to tell me something good before we get done here."

Nina checked her watch. "Okay, but I don't have too long. So, go ahead. Tell me what's up?"

The server came to take their order, and once he'd gone Nina raised an eyebrow at Teresa. "What's going on?"

"Elle's boyfriend's been cheating on her. He's walked out on her and little Skye."

"Oh, no! What's she going to do?"

"The only thing she can do. She's coming home."

"Oh, wow. To stay with you?"

Teresa nodded. "I'm her only choice. Of course, I'll love having them, but Elle's miserable. She doesn't know what she's going to do. I've told her we'll figure it out. She could come in the salon with me, but … well, you can imagine how she feels about that."

Nina nodded. Teresa's daughter Elle had gone down to the city to train as a stylist. She'd said she planned to come home and work with her mom, but she'd met a guy and had a beautiful little girl with him.

"I'm glad she's coming, though. I thought she might try to make it on her own down there. But I hate the thought of Skye being watched by strangers while she works. Here, we can figure it out between us. And selfishly, it means I'll get to know my granddaughter and be a part of her life."

"Yeah, that's a bright side."

The server came back with their food.

"Anyway," said Teresa once he'd gone. "That's my news. And you promised me something good. What's happening with you and Manny?"

Nina smiled. "It's all good. The whole Brian thing is behind me. We had dinner with Abbie and Ivan the other night and that went really well. I felt like we were all a family."

"Aww. That's lovely. And are you going to make it official?"

"What do you mean?"

Teresa laughed. "You know what I mean. Are you going make him part of the family—marry him?"

Nina's heart raced. "Oh. I don't know about that. He … he wants us to get a place together." She'd kept pushing that thought away since he'd mentioned it on Sunday. She didn't love her house. If she were honest, she'd rather move out of it and start fresh in a new place with Manny, but she couldn't afford to. Even if she sold her place, there wouldn't be much left after all the old debts were paid off. The way she saw it, the house was the only thing she brought to the table.

"So, why don't you? You can't tell me you want to stay in your house?"

"No, I don't really, but …"

"You think you might need to hold on to it? In case things don't work out?"

"No. It's not that. It's just … he wanted to go and look over at Four Mile. I can't afford even the smallest place over there."

Teresa held her gaze.

"What?"

"Does he expect you to?"

"Whether he expects it or not, that's not the point."

"Why not? He came here thinking that he might stay—that he might buy a house. I'd guess that somewhere over there would be his kind of place—his kind of price range. Are you saying that if he wants to be with you, he has to be prepared to go down market?" She smiled to soften her words. "You know I'm not being a bitch. I'm just being honest about it."

Nina nodded grudgingly. "I know. And you're right. I didn't think that was what I was doing, but you kind of have a point."

"Good. I'm glad I got through to you. And for what it's worth, I don't think it'd matter much to Manny if he lived in a little place like yours or one of the big waterfront estates—not for the sake of the house. But I don't think it's fair to ask him to move into the house that you and Paul shared for all those years." She frowned. "I know it's none of my damned business, but please tell me that you're not sleeping in the *bed* you and Paul shared?"

Nina had to laugh at the look on her friend's face. "No. We're not. It really is none of your business, but we sleep in Abbie's room."

Teresa smiled. "See, even you know that it'd be weird to ask him to sleep in Paul's bed. Don't you think it's weird to ask him to live in Paul's house?"

Nina sighed. "You're right. I know it is. I just ... I don't want him to see me as some needy female who he not only needs to protect, but also needs to provide for."

Teresa laughed. "I'd guess that that's exactly what he wants to do. And there's nothing wrong with it. I know you. I'll bet you provide for him in different ways. You take care of him, feed him, don't you?"

"Yeah."

"You don't see him as needy because of it, do you?"

"No."

"So why not be a be a team with him? Cover each other's weaknesses. Let him provide what you can't and you do the same for him?"

"I guess."

"Think about it, at least?"

"I will. Thanks, Tere."

"You're welcome. And as always, feel free to ignore me. I only stick my nose in because I care and I want to see you happy." Teresa checked her watch. "And I've talked too much and kept you too long. Go on. I'll stay and get the check. You get back to work. Will I see you at the weekend?"

"Thanks." Nina got to her feet. "I don't know. I'll call you. I told you that Manny's ex-wife and her husband—his friend—are coming?"

"Damn! You did, and I so wanted to ask you about that. But you need to go."

"Yeah. I'll call you. Maybe you can come out with us all—see what you make of it. It all sounds good, but it'll be interesting to see."

"I'm there if you need me." Teresa smiled. "I've got your back."

Nina went around the table to hug her before she left. "I don't know how I went all that time without you."

Teresa hugged her back. "You didn't. I've been here for you since we were kids. I always will be."

~ ~ ~

Manny couldn't settle on Saturday while they waited for Andrés and Kim to arrive. He checked his watch and then went back into the living room. When he got there, he couldn't remember why—or if he'd even had a reason to go in there. He came back into the kitchen and stopped when he realized that Nina was watching him with a smile playing on her lips.

"What?"

She chuckled. "You're nervous."

He was, but he didn't want to tell her why. "What makes you think that?"

"You're pacing. You do that when you're agitated."

He frowned. "I never told you that."

"You didn't need to. You're not the only one with powers of observation, you know."

He folded his arms across his chest and leaned against the doorframe. "Sorry."

She came to him and slipped her arms around his waist. "Don't be. But don't worry. There's nothing to be nervous about. I won't embarrass you."

He lowered his head to hers until he was looking deep into her eyes. His hand came up and closed around the back of her neck as he drew her to him for a kiss.

"Wow!" she breathed when he finally lifted his head. "What was that for?"

"For being you. For being so clueless."

She laughed. "Thanks. I think. What am I being clueless about?"

"Everything! You think I'm nervous about what they'll think?" He shook his head adamantly. "Nope. I'm nervous what you'll think. They've been my friends for most of life. I want you to like them."

Her cheeks flushed. "Aww. I didn't even think of it that way around."

He dropped a peck on her lips. "I know, that's one of the reasons that I—"

The doorbell rang, interrupting him. It seemed that any time he was about to tell her how he felt, something came up to stop him. He was determined now, though. Perhaps this wasn't the best time with his friends arriving, but before this weekend was over he needed to tell her that he loved her—and that he wasn't just excited about them starting a new chapter of life together, but that he was hoping she'd want to spend the rest of her life with him.

She was looking up at him. "We should get the door."

He let out a half laugh. "I know. But I still feel ... this is your house."

She made a face, but he wasn't making a point about it. He honestly didn't feel that it was his place to let people into her home.

She took hold of his hand and they went together. "You're right," she said before she opened the door. "After they've gone, we need to talk about where we're going to live."

His heart raced. "You want to?" he asked eagerly.

"Yeah. I do. I don't want be here any more than you do." She reached to open the door, but he caught her lips in a kiss first, then brushed his thumb over them.

"I promise I'll do everything I can to make you happy."

She chuckled. "You already do, but for now, you should probably let me open the door." As she spoke, the doorbell rang again, and they both laughed.

Half an hour later, the four of them were sitting out on the patio behind the house. Manny was loving this, every minute of it. Nina and Kim chatted as if they'd been friends for ever.

Andrés caught his eye and smiled. "So, you're going to be working part-time? What are you going to be doing, or shouldn't I ask?"

Manny smiled. "You can ask, but I can't tell you or, if I did, I'd have to shoot you."

"Just the same as before, then?"

Manny shrugged. "Kind of. Not really. It's security work. Dan's already set up his cyber security operation. He doesn't need me for that; it's not my area of expertise. I can manage the teams, but I can't do what they do."

"What will you be doing, then?" asked Kim. "What kind of security?"

He looked at Nina when he spoke. "Helping out when people have problems that they need taking care of. Protection duties, that kind of thing."

She'd told him that if his work was secret, she didn't want to ask him about it, but he wondered if she had questions and if she'd ask them now.

She smiled. "And that *is* your area of expertise."

He chuckled. "I guess you could say that."

Kim smiled at Nina. "I imagine it didn't take you very long to figure out that that's not just what he does, it's who he is."

Nina nodded. "I don't imagine it takes anyone who ever meets him very long."

Kim laughed. "No, you've got a point there, but it's different. I couldn't stand it." She made a face at Manny and he and Andres laughed remembering so many fights. Kim ignored them and continued talking to Nina. "We're different, though, you and me. I was Manny's worst nightmare, bless him. But you, it's so obvious you're his dream come true. We worried that we'd never see him fall for someone. Never see him love someone the way he loves you. It's so wonderful."

Manny's heart thudded to a halt. His eyes darted toward Nina. She looked as shocked as he felt. Perhaps she wasn't ready to hear it. Maybe it was too soon, and Kim had gone and blown it. He hadn't told them that he loved Nina, but apparently, it was blatantly obvious.

Andrés cleared his throat and spoke into the awkward silence that had fallen around the table. "Do you work, Nina?"

She turned to look at him as if he'd just spoken in Chinese or some other foreign tongue she didn't understand, but then she pulled herself together and smiled. "I do. I work at the gift store at the resort."

Manny got to his feet. "I'll get some more drinks." He needed a minute. Every time he thought things were moving along well, something came up to make him question whether he wasn't rushing too much.

He went inside and grasped the counter with both hands, dropping his head and closing his eyes as he hoped that Nina's reaction had simply been shock to hear Kim say it so openly when he hadn't said those words himself yet.

He looked up when the door opened, and Kim came in. "I am so freaking sorry! But give me a clue, Manny! She doesn't know that you love her? How have you not told her? How can she not see it?"

He shrugged. "I don't seem to be handling it too well. I haven't had much practice."

"Maybe not, but you're a fast learner. Jeez, Manny. You need to tell her. And if I know you, you're not one hundred percent sure of how she feels, are you?"

He shook his head. "Not completely."

She let out a short laugh. "Well, you can be. She's as head over heels in love with you as you are with her. So, why don't you just tell her. Tell her everything you feel, everything you want and get on and marry her."

"Marry her?"

"Yes. Marry her, why not?"

Manny held her gaze for a long moment. "Why not indeed?"

Nina tried to focus on what Andrés was saying. She liked him. She could see why he and Manny were friends. But she couldn't keep her mind on the conversation. Kim thought Manny loved her? It shouldn't be such a shock. Perhaps it wasn't, really. Perhaps the shock was only from hearing someone else say it before they'd had a chance to themselves.

"Don't you think?"

She realized Andrés was watching her, waiting for her to answer, but she had no clue what he was talking about.

He smiled. "I'm sorry about that. Kim shouldn't have said anything."

She smiled back at him. "It's okay."

He nodded. "They're just friends, you know. I hope it doesn't bother you … how close they are."

"No! It really doesn't. It's not that, it's just …" She glanced at the kitchen door. Kim had followed Manny in there. She was no doubt apologizing. Nina didn't think for a minute that she'd had any ill intentions. She'd simply put her foot in it, and the look on her face had said she felt terrible about it. She let out a small laugh. "Perhaps she did us a favor. Manny and I haven't exactly done too well with making our feelings clear. We've been too busy trying not to mess things up."

"I don't think you could mess things up, no matter how hard you tried. You're perfect for each other, and Kim shouldn't have said it, but it's obvious that you love each other very much."

She nodded.

"Are there any real reasons for you to hold back?"

She shook her head slowly. "No, there are details that we need to work out, but that's all."

"You'll work them out. I know you will. And I think we should take off now. Give the two of you the chance to talk."

"You don't need to."

He smiled. "I think we do."

They looked up when Manny came back outside. He came to Nina and squatted down beside her chair, taking both her hands in his. "I'm sorry."

"Don't you dare!"

He chuckled. "I can't help it. I am."

She touched his face. "I'm sorry, too."

Andrés got to his feet when Kim came out. "We'll see you guys soon."

"But you can't just—" Nina felt bad that they would leave so suddenly, but Manny just nodded.

"Thanks, guys. You're staying over at Four Mile, right?"

"Yes." Kim gave Nina an apologetic smile. "We're here till tomorrow afternoon."

"If you want to call," said Andrés. "Don't worry if you don't. We'll see you next time." He went and took Kim's hand and led her to the side gate.

Nina started to get to her feet. They should go and say goodbye to them, but Manny kept hold of her hands and didn't move. He just called, "See you, guys."

Once they'd gone, he got up and tugged on her hands for her to go with him. He led her inside and sat down on the sofa, pulling her down into his lap.

He closed his arms around her and covered her mouth in a kiss that left her breathless

When he lifted his head, he brushed his thumb over her lips. "I love you."

Her breath caught in her chest, and tears pricked behind her eyes. "I love you, too."

He brushed his lips over hers. "I'm sorry, I—"

She chuckled. "If we're going to live together, then I'm going to have to ask you not to keep apologizing."

His eyebrows came down. "I'm sorry, I …" He rolled his eyes. "I can't help it. I love you so damned much. It makes me stupid. That's the only way I can explain it to myself. I've messed up pretty much every step of the way."

"No. You haven't messed anything up. We've both been wary, that's all. I've wanted to tell you, too."

His eyes shone happily. "You have?"

She nodded. "I've known for a little while now. I love you, Manny."

"I love you more." He claimed her mouth in another kiss that left her in no doubt.

Chapter Twenty

Manny rubbed his sweaty palms on his jeans as he walked across the plaza at Four Mile with Andrés. Today had been a crazy day, but he was hoping that it would be the happiest day of his life.

He was finally relaxed about where he and Nina were headed. He wasn't entirely sure that she'd want to get married. But he hoped she would. They'd talked for hours last night after Kim and Andrés had left. He was relieved that she'd told him all about what Paul had done and what her life with him had been like. Of course, he'd already known. But he was glad that she'd told him herself. Plus, she'd given him the story behind the facts that Ivan had shared. That helped him understand her better. He knew now that he'd have to make sure that she was honest with him about what she wanted. He didn't want her to go along with whatever he said.

He'd told her about his marriage to Kim. There were no horror stories, but it hadn't been a happy time in his life. They did great now as friends, but their relationship as a couple hadn't been healthy. It'd left him believing that he wasn't cut out to be with a woman, certainly not to be married. But now he knew better. He was cut out to be with Nina and he wanted nothing more than to be married to her.

That was the reason he and Andrés were heading to the jewelry store where Maria worked. Nina and Kim were meeting up with Teresa and Audrey and Izzy at the café. They'd run into Ted and Audrey this morning while they were driving around the development at Four Mile Creek. Ted and Audrey had built a house there and had told them about one that had just come on the market. It wasn't a new build; it was a resale down on the water's edge. He smiled. It had a pool. And after what Nina had told him last night he'd already decided that whatever house they bought would have to have a pool.

Andrés grasped his shoulder. "You look intense."

He chuckled. "I feel it. I have to get this right."

"You will. You already got it right. She's perfect for you."

"She is. I know it. I meant the ring."

Andrés laughed. "Perhaps you should have brought Kim instead of me."

"No. That was about the only thing I knew about choosing this ring. It's not Kim's place. I don't want her to be part of it. I don't think Nina would care, but it seems wrong to me."

"Yeah. I can see that. I'll do my best."

They reached the store and Manny held the door open for his friend to go in ahead of him.

Maria came around the counter and greeted him with a hug. "Hey, you! I'm so excited!"

"Me, too. But I'm nervous."

She waved a hand at him. "There's no need. That's what you've got me for."

The door from the back opened and Zack came out with a big grin on his face. "And me. I want to say I was part of this." He turned around as someone else came out behind him.

"Ryan?" Manny laughed. "Don't tell me you have a sudden interest in engagement rings?"

"Nah. But I ran into Zack this morning and he told me what was going on and …" He shrugged. "Okay. I admit it. I wanted to be part of it, too. I never thought I'd see the day."

"Me neither." He looked around at the three men. "Thanks guys." Then he turned to Maria. "I'm depending on you. Where do we start?"

She smiled and pulled out a tray. "I got you a selection so we can start to narrow it down."

Manny's heart thundered in his chest. He couldn't believe he was actually doing this.

~ ~ ~

It was early evening by the time they got back to the house. Nina was exhausted. It'd been a long day after a night of not much sleep. It had been a fun day, though.

Abbie and Ivan had stopped by this morning which had been a nice surprise. She didn't know what they were up to, but they'd had some whispered discussion with Manny in the living room while they all thought she was busy in the kitchen. It didn't matter what they were up to. She loved that the three of them got along so well already.

She plonked herself down on a stool at the counter. Manny came and slid his arms around her waist and kissed the back of her neck. "Do you want to go and get comfortable on one of the loungers outside? I know you like to enjoy the last of the sun. I'll bring you a drink out. I just have to do a couple things."

She leaned back against him and sighed happily. "Have I told you lately how wonderful you are? That sounds perfect. I'll go just as soon as I work up the energy."

He came around and scooped her off the stool. "No energy needed. I'll take you."

He deposited her on the lounger and dropped a kiss on her lips. "I'll be out in a few. What do you want to drink?"

"Just a water, thanks."

"I'll be right out."

She watched him go and then closed her eyes and enjoyed the feel of the last warm rays of the sun on her face. It'd been a busy day, but a wonderful one. If this was what her new life was going to be like, she couldn't be happier. After Ivan and Abbie left, they'd gone over to Four Mile Creek. They'd only planned to drive around and get an idea what the houses were like and seeing them had convinced her that she had no reason at all to get silly about holding onto this place. Running into Audrey and Ted had been good too. It'd be wonderful to have them as neighbors and they'd told them about the place down on the water.

She hugged herself. She couldn't help it. The thought of living in that house with Manny was amazing. It was right on the water. The views were amazing. The kitchen made her feel like she might have died and gone to heaven. And she'd teared up when she'd seen the pool and Manny had told her that no matter what house they got, she was going to get her pool.

She opened her eyes and looked up at the sky. It was going to be a beautiful sunset. She hoped Manny wouldn't be too long. She wanted him to enjoy it, too.

He came out carrying a tray and set it down on the table between the two loungers. He gave her a glass of water and she noticed that his hand was trembling.

"Are you okay?"

He nodded and sat down opposite her. "I am."

She gave him a stern look. "What's going on with you? You know you can't fool me."

He chuckled, but his tension didn't go away. "I have … I want … Oh, screw it." He reached for an envelope that was on the tray he'd brought out. "Remember this?" He handed it to her.

It took her a moment to realize that it was the note he'd written and then mailed the first weekend he was here. "I do. This was your hunch when we first met. Am I allowed to read it now?"

He nodded. "I'd like you to."

She tore it open, but couldn't tear her gaze away from his. This felt important. Monumental was the word that came to mind.

She held the piece of note paper for a moment until he nodded, and she looked down at it and started to read.

Nina

I know if I said this to you right now, it'd scare you. You've just escaped from one scary guy. I don't want you to think that I'm another. But I do want to tell you how I feel.

I just kissed you for the first time and I told you that our first kiss would not be our last. As soon as I said that I got a strong feeling that we'd both just had our last first kiss—ever.

Nina's eyes filled with tears and she looked up at him. "Our last first kiss."

He nodded. "God, I hope so, Nina. You're it for me."

She squeezed his hand. "You're it for me, too, Manny."

She looked back down at the note in her hands, wondering what else he'd known back then but hadn't dared to say—maybe even to believe.

Last night, at the Boathouse I told you I'd be happy to rescue you and that I had the feeling that you might be the one to rescue me. If you're reading this, then you can know that I'll come to your rescue whenever you need me from anything big or small, for the rest of your days. And you can also know that you rescued me. You rescued me from becoming that lonely soul who rode off into the sunset—alone. That's how I saw retirement.

I first saw you at sunset. You didn't know I was here. I parked outside and you were nothing more than a beautiful silhouette in the window. Until that moment, I didn't think I wanted a woman in my life. When I saw you, I knew I did. I wanted you before I even knew who you were.

If you're reading this, then we'll both know my hunch, my feeling about us was right. We're going to live out our sunset years together.

If I've timed this right, then you should be able to look up and see a beautiful sunset.

She looked up at the sky that was turning crimson and gold and then at Manny again. Tears were streaming down her face. He brushed them away with his thumb and nodded for her to continue.

You've already told me about some shadows that life has cast on you. I want you to know that I'll shine the light into every dark corner, until there are no shadows left. You deserve only sunshine.

I believe that you've changed my life. I hope you'll allow me to change yours.

I hope you get to read this, and I hope that by the time you do, I'll have found the perfect way to tell you.

I love you.

Manny.

She couldn't hold in the sob that escaped as she flung her arms around his neck. "Manny!"

He crushed her to his chest. "You would have thought I was crazy if I'd said it."

She sniffed and leaned back to look at him. "You're right. I would. But I'm so glad you wrote it down. I love you, Manny, so much."

"I love you more."

"I'll treasure that note forever. Can I tell Abbie?"

"You can."

"She'll love it so much. She loves that we're together, you know."

He smiled and took hold of her hand. "I do know. She told me this morning when I talked to her and Ivan."

Nina wiped her eyes. "Yeah, what was that about?"

His big brown eyes were so full of love as he slid down from the lounger and got on one knee.

Her heart started to race as she understood what he was doing.

"It was about this. I needed to know that she'd be okay with it if I asked you."

Nina's hand came up to cover her mouth.

He held up a ring box with a beautiful diamond solitaire ring in it. "Nina. Will you marry me? I love you with all my heart.

People used to joke that maybe I didn't have one. But since I met you, I know that I do and it's so full of love for you. I promise I'll love you for the rest of my days. I'll take care of you, I'll protect you and I'll do everything I can to help you be more of you." He looked so uncertain when he looked up into her eyes. "Do you want to be my wife?"

"Yes!" Tears were streaming down her face again as she got down on her knees with him and cupped his face between her hands. "There's nothing in the world I want more than to be your wife. To call you my husband and to love you till the day I die."

He closed his arms around her, and they kissed as the sun set;

;

I hope you enjoyed Nina and Manny's story. You probably noticed that there were a few characters in there angling for a story of their own. (As always!) Well, I'm happy to tell you that Leanne and Ryan have elbowed their way to the front of the line. Their story has been a long time coming – we first met them back in Dance Like Nobody's Watching. It won't be much longer now though. It'll be out later this year – that's SJ speak for I'm not sure when yet ;0)

You can check out the latest on Summer Lake at my website for more details.

A Note from SJ

I hope you enjoyed Nina and Manny's story. Please let your friends know about the books if you feel they would enjoy them as well. It would be wonderful if you would leave me a review, I'd very much appreciate it.

Check out the "Also By" page to see if any of my other series appeal to you – I have a couple of ebook freebie series starters, too, so you can take them for a test drive.

There are a few options to keep up with me and my imaginary friends:

The best way is to Sign up for my Newsletter at my website www.SJMcCoy.com. Don't worry I won't bombard you! I'll let you know about upcoming releases, share a sneak peek or two and keep you in the loop for a couple of fun giveaways I have coming up :0)

You can join my readers group to chat about the books or like my Facebook Page   www.facebook.com/authorsjmccoy
I occasionally attempt to say something in 140 characters or less(!) on Twitter

And I'm in the process of building a shiny new website at www.SJMcCoy.com

I love to hear from readers, so feel free to email me at SJ@SJMcCoy.com if you'd like. I'm better at that! :0)

I hope our paths will cross again soon. Until then, take care, and thanks for your support—you are the reason I write!

Love

SJ

PS Project Semicolon

You may have noticed that the final sentence of the story closed with a semi-colon. It isn't a typo. <u>Project Semi Colon</u> is a non-profit movement dedicated to presenting hope and love to those who are struggling with depression, suicide, addiction and self-injury. Project Semicolon exists to encourage, love and inspire. It's a movement I support with all my heart.

"A semicolon represents a sentence the author could have ended, but chose not to. The sentence is your life and the author is you." - Project Semicolon

This author started writing after her son was killed in a car crash. At the time I wanted my own story to be over, instead I chose to honour a promise to my son to write my 'silly stories' someday. I chose to escape into my fictional world. I know for many who struggle with depression, suicide can appear to be the only escape. The semicolon has become a symbol of support, and hopefully a reminder – Your story isn't over yet

Also by SJ McCoy

Summer Lake Silver

Clay and Marianne in Like Some Old Country Song

Seymour and Chris in A Dream Too Far

Ted and Audrey in A Little Rain Must Fall

Izzy and Diego in Where the Rainbow Ends

Summer Lake Seasons

Angel and Luke in Take These Broken Wings

Zack and Maria in Too Much Love to Hide

Logan and Roxy in Sunshine Over Snow

Ivan and Abbie in Chase the Blues Away

Colt and Cassie in Forever Takes a While

Summer Lake Series

Love Like You've Never Been Hurt (FREE in ebook form)

Work Like You Don't Need the Money

Dance Like Nobody's Watching

Fly Like You've Never Been Grounded

Laugh Like You've Never Cried

Sing Like Nobody's Listening

Smile Like You Mean It

The Wedding Dance

Chasing Tomorrow

Dream Like Nothing's Impossible

Ride Like You've Never Fallen

Live Like There's No Tomorrow

The Wedding Flight

Remington Ranch Series
Mason (FREE in ebook form) and also available as Audio
Shane
Carter
Beau
Four Weddings and a Vendetta

A Chance and a Hope
Chance is a guy with a whole lot of story to tell. He's part of the fabric of both Summer Lake and Remington Ranch. He needed three whole books to tell his own story.

Chance Encounter
Finding Hope
Give Hope a Chance

Love in Nashville
Autumn and Matt in Bring on the Night

The Davenports
Oscar
TJ
Reid

The Hamiltons
Cameron and Piper in Red wine and Roses
Chelsea and Grant in Champagne and Daisies
Mary Ellen and Antonio in Marsala and Magnolias
Marcos and Molly in Prosecco and Peonies
Coming Next
Grady

About the Author

I'm SJ, a coffee addict, lover of chocolate and drinker of good red wines. I'm a lost soul and a hopeless romantic. Reading and writing are necessary parts of who I am. Though perhaps not as necessary as coffee! I can drink coffee without writing, but I can't write without coffee.

I grew up loving romance novels, my first boyfriends were book boyfriends, but life intervened, as it tends to do, and I wandered down the paths of non-fiction for many years. My life changed completely a few years ago and I returned to Romance to find my escape.

I write 'Sweet n Steamy' stories because to me there is enough angst and darkness in real life. My favorite romances are happy escapes with a focus on fun, friendships and happily-ever-afters, just like the ones I write.

These days I live in beautiful Montana, the last best place. If I'm not reading or writing, you'll find me just down the road in the park - Yellowstone. I have deer, eagles and the occasional bear for company, and I like it that way :0)

Printed in Great Britain
by Amazon